Praise For
THE BLUESUIT CHRONICLES

"Your book would make an excellent TV series. It features police work from the vantagepoint of the policeman, emphasizing the exposure to the danger of police work, as you carefully work around the restraints set forth in the law. I know the public does not realize what the cop is up-against, and this book sets forth that scenario without fault. The major bestseller *The New Centurions*, by Joseph Wambaugh, is a book I will never forget, and your book is equal to his."
~Patrick Lowe, Anderson Island, WA

"The first installment of The Bluesuit Chronicles, *(The War Comes Home)* is a compelling start to what is sure to be an epic saga. A former Golden Gloves boxer and Army medic returns home from Vietnam to a very different America than the one he left. The drug craze of the early seventies takes a heavy toll on the Boomer generation, and the social fabric begins to unravel, nail-biting action, romance, and intrigue, based on actual events." Rated Four Stars.
~ Red City Reviews

"An exciting, read, riveting action, romance and moving scenes. *The War Comes Home* took me back to the Bellevue I knew in 'the good old days.' Impossible to put down." ~ Cynthia Davis, Bellevue, WA

"*The War Comes Home* follows the activities of two city police officers, Hitchcock and Walker, as they prepare and then head out for the nightly patrol of their Neighborhood streets. Hitchcock feels a strange foreboding that there will be danger that evening, and someone will die. The two police officers spend the evening patrolling areas looking for drug dealers, prostitutes, and other criminals.
This manuscript is extremely well-written. The author has infused the prose with an interesting mix of dialogue, inner thoughts. The characters are nicely developed, the dialogue is genuine and flows organically. The reader is immediately drawn into the story and wants to learn more, not only about the officers, but what awaits them as they begin their nightly patrol." ~ Editor at Bookbaby

Praise For
THE BLUESUIT CHRONICLES

"Having grown up in Bellevue in the '60s and '70s, I bought the entire series for my husband for his birthday. He is completely engrossed in them. Thank you, John, for writing them, it's hard to get him to relax, and the books are doing it with laughter and 'do you remember' comments. We are eagerly waiting for the next book to come out."
~ Jeanie Hack, Bellevue, WA

"From the moment I started reading *The War Comes Home*, I couldn't put it down. I was captivated by the balance of action and drama that John Hansen expertly weaves throughout this fast-paced historical fiction. I'm looking forward to reading the next one."
~ S. McDonald, Redmond, WA

"Book Two of The Bluesuit Chronicles series, *The New Darkness*, continues the story of Vietnam veteran Roger Hitchcock, now a police officer in Bellevue, Washington. The spreading new drug culture is taking a heavy toll on Hitchcock's generation. Some die, some are permanently impaired, everyone is impacted by this wave of evil that even turns traditional values inside out. Like other officer, the times test Hitchcock: will he resign in disgust, become hardened and bitter, corrupt, or will his background in competition boxing and military combat experience enable him to rise to meet the challenge? Romance, intrigue and action are the fabric of *The New Darkness*."
~ Amazon.com

"*Valley of Long Shadows* is the third book in The Bluesuit Chronicles… Returning Vietnam veterans who become police officers find themselves holding the line against societal anarchy. Even traditional roles between cops and robbers in police work have become more deadly…The backdrop is one of government betrayal, societal breakdown, and an angry disillusioned public. The '70s is the decade that brought America where it is now.
Four Stars Rating ~ Red City Reviews

Praise For
THE BLUESUIT CHRONICLES

"By the time I finished reading the series up through Book Four (*Day Shift*), I concluded most men would like to be Hitchcock, at least in some way. What sets him apart is the dichotomy of his makeup: he grew up with a Boy Scout sense of honor and right and wrong, yet he isn't hardened or jaded by the evil and cruelty he saw when he went to war, though he killed in combat. As a policeman he *chooses* good and right: to do otherwise is unthinkable. He is a skilled fighter, yet so modest that he doesn't know he is a role model for others around him, and women feel safe with him. I know Hitchcock's type—two of my relatives were cops who influenced my life:"
~ Tracy Smith, Newcastle, WA

"Book Five (*Unfinished Business*) moves to show how difficult it is for Officer Hitchcock to do right. Bad people are out to get him for his good work. He is a threat to their nefarious activities. There is even a very bad high-ranking policeman who puts Hitchcock and his family in extreme peril. Organized foreign crime is moving into his city, he works hard to uncover the clues to solve this evil in his city. I'm still waiting to find out what restaurant owner Juju is up to and who she works for. Great series and story. Another fine book by John Hansen. Yo! ~ T.A. Smith

"I've read all of John's books and rated them all 5 stars, because those stars are earned. I worked the street with John as a police officer for years and what he speaks of in his books is real. John is an excellent author; articulate and clear, always bringing the reader directly into the story. I like John's work to the point that I've asked him to send me any new books he writes; I'll be either the first or almost the first to read all of them. I lived this with John. He's an author not to be missed. You can't go wrong reading his books. I strongly encourage more in the series." ~ Bill Cooper, Chief of Police (ret)

Praise For
THE BLUESUIT CHRONICLES

"John Hansen has written another great read. *Unfinished Business* is filled with conspiracy, corruption and crime, much of which is targeted at Hitchcock. From the beginning of the book, I was hooked. The author has a gift with words that drew me into the story effortlessly— I could not put the book down. I have read all in the series and I look forward to reading more of John Hansen's books." ~ S. McDonald

"A viewpoint from the inside: I worked with and partnered with John both in uniform and in detectives, and like him I came to the Department after military service. This is the fifth (as of this date) of five books in this series. I have read and re-read all five books, and for the first time, recently, over a two-day period, read the entire series in order. All five books were inspired by John's experiences, during many of which I was present. John is an extremely gifted author and I was transported back to those times and experienced a full gamut of emotions, mostly good, sometimes less so. His use of humor, love, anger, fear, camaraderie, loyalty, respect, disapproval, devotion, and other emotions, rang true throughout the books." ~ Robert Littlejohn

"The whole series of The Bluesuit Chronicles brought back a flood of memories. I started in police work in 1976. This series starts a couple of years earlier. The descriptions of the equipment, the way you had to solve crimes without the assistance of modern items. John made me feel that I was there when it was happening. This whole series is what police work is about. Working with citizens, caring about them, and catching the bad guys. Officers in that time period cared about what they did. It wasn't all about a paycheck… We were the originators of community policing. We knew our beat and the people in it. I am not saying we were perfect; however, we were very committed to our community. That being said, I can't wait for the next book. Please read the whole series. Once you start you won't stop."
~ Garry C. Dixon, Ret. LEO-Virginia

Praise For
THE BLUESUIT CHRONICLES

"Received Book 4, *Day Shift* on a Wednesday. Already done reading it. Couldn't help myself. Was only going to read a couple chapters and save the rest for my upcoming camping trip. LOL. 3 hours later book finished. Love it. 2 Thumbs up !!! ~ Alanda Bailey, Kalispell, MT

"Retired Detective John Hansen is a master writer. He brings to life policing in the Northwestern U.S. during the '70s; a transitional period. One has to wonder of how much of his writings are founded in personal experience vs. creative thinking. Either way, his stories are thoroughly enjoyable and well-worth purchasing his original books in this series, his current release, as well as the books yet to come."
~ Debbie M.-Scottsdale, AZ

"I urge you to complete your 'to do' list prior to reading *Unfinished Business*, as once started, I could not put it down. It was always, 'one more page' and soon I was not getting anything else done, but it was well worth it. The author has an amazing way of drawing the reader into each scene, adding to the excitement, sweet romance, raw emotion and revealing of each fascinating character as the plots unfold. I highly recommend this book to anyone who wants a truly good read. Looking forward to the next book from this highly talented author." ~ Cynthia R.

"I received the 5th book in The Bluesuit Chronicles and started reading and per usual, didn't stop until I finished the book. I am a huge fan of John's stories. I grew up in the general area that the stories are set in. Also, in the same time frame. John's books are always fast paced and entertaining reads. I would recommend them to any and all."
~ A. Bailey-Kalispell, MT

Also by John Hansen:

The Award -Winning Series: The Bluesuit Chronicles:

The War Comes Home
The New Darkness
Valley of Long Shadows
Day Shift
Unfinished Business
The Mystery of the Unseen Hand

Published & Award -Winning Essays and Short Stories:

"Losing Kristene"
"Riding the Superstitions"
"The Case of the Old Colt"
"Charlie's Story"
"The Mystery of Three"
"The Prospector"

Non-Fiction Book:
Song of the Waterwheel

The War Comes Home

Book 1 of The Bluesuit Chronicles

JOHN HANSEN

The War Comes Home
by John Hansen

This book is a work of fiction. Names, characters, locations and
events are either a product of the author's imagination, fictitious or
used fictitiously. Any resemblance to any event, locale or person,
living or dead, is purely coincidental.

Third Edition
Revised and Reprinted - Copyright © 2020 John Hansen
Original Copyright © 2017 John Hansen

Cover Designer: Jessica Bell - Jessica Bell Design
Interior Design and Formatting: Deborah J Ledford - IOF Productions Ltd

Issued in Print and Electronic Formats
Trade Paperback ISBN: 978-1735803005

Manufactured in the United States of America

The War Comes Home

JOHN HANSEN

To Patricia, my wife,
whose amazing love and beauty, inside and out,
have given me a fresh start in life.

From the Author

Many of the events in *The War Comes Home* are based on my personal experiences as a young police officer who returned home in 1970 after four years military service which involved two one-year tours in and around Vietnam. The first half of my twenty-one years on the Bellevue, Washington Police Department were in the Patrol Division. I was a detective during the remaining years.

The dramatic changes in our country over the past few decades led to the realization that when I became a cop, I was on the front lines at the beginning of a defining decade for America. I decided I had better start writing about it to preserve it for future generations.

By 2012 I had written my first book, *Song of the Waterwheel*, in honor of my late wife of 28 years, whom I lost to cancer. It was after this that I felt the urge to document the decade, the era from the perspective of those of us who left home and family to serve, and continued to do the same when we returned to a self-destructive mess at home. I write The Bluesuit Chronicles series, based on my experiences and observations, in a re-created historical setting

I have enjoyed writing the series in a one-book-leads-to-the-next manner, involving the same characters who progress through the decade together. The main character, Roger Hitchcock, and the three fellow officers closest to him, are adventurous types who have a sort of "Three Musketeers" camaraderie sense of good fellowship. "All for one, and one for all."

Enjoy the ride,
John Hansen

FOREWORD

FBI field agents of the '60s and '70s coined the term "bluesuits" when referring to non-federal law enforcement officers, whether city, county or state cops, uniformed or plain clothes. For them it was a handy in-house term when they worked with us often during a time of exploding crime. Assaults, bombings, attacks on government buildings, prison and jail breaks, kidnappings, robberies and homicides rose to levels not seen since the aftermath of the Civil War. Serial rapists and killers who crossed state lines burst upon the scene, and assassinations—in the form of deadly frontal attacks and ambushes of bluesuits reached unprecedented levels.

The Bureau's statistics revealed a shocking truth regarding officers who were killed in the line of duty from 1971 through 1974. *Over half* were members of suburban or small-town police departments and rural "cow county" sheriff's offices. The common characteristics were lower expectations of serious trouble, lower training and hiring standards, which, combined with the dullness of routine patrol, led to deadly complacency, which often resulted in crippling injuries or police funerals.

The Bluesuit Chronicles are based largely on my own experiences as a cop during the '70s, to tell the untold story of those of us who were cops in the shadows of our brother officers in the big cities.

See, I will make you into a threshing sledge, new and sharp, with many teeth. You will thresh the mountains and crush them, and reduce the hills to chaff. You will winnow them, the wind will pick them up, and a gale will blow them away. But you will rejoice in the Lord and glory in the Holy One of Israel.

~ Isaiah 41:15-16

PROLOGUE

South Vietnam, 1969

NINE SPECIAL FORCES soldiers endured sweltering tropical heat as they crept in single file across an open field, hidden from view by elephant grass five to seven feet tall called "wait a minute grass" by American GI's.

In case of enemy snipers or capture, they wore no insignias or indications of rank. Leafy vegetation attached to their uniforms, short-brimmed Boonie hats, and dark grease smeared on their faces, necks and hands made them almost invisible to enemy eyes.

Sweat from heat, stagnant air and humidity darkened their uniforms. To minimize quick hand movements which could catch the eyes of enemy sentries, they tied strips of camouflage cloth around their heads to stop sweat from running into their eyes.

The point man, a square-jawed corporal the men called The Virginian, suddenly raised his hand shoulder-high and dropped to a squat. The men behind him knelt in their tracks. The officer in charge, a new man, and the sergeant approached.

The Virginian unsheathed his bayonet as he pointed to an out-of-place bundle of long sharp-bladed grasses and tree leaves on the path ahead; a camouflage flaw only a veteran would spot.

"Trayap, suhr," he said, his Southern drawl barely above a whisper. He carefully lifted the grasses away first with the tip of his bayonet, then the leaves that didn't belong there, exposing a dozen sharp punji sticks pointing upright from the bottom of a square pit two feet deep.

Amazed, the officer looked to the sergeant. "A trap here means the VC are within earshot of us, sir," the sergeant whispered.

The officer shrugged, indicating he didn't understand.

"The screams of a soldier falling onto punji sticks would alert the VC of our location, sir," the sergeant explained, "we're so exposed here, they'd slaughter us in seconds."

The officer acknowledged with a nod, then signaled to move on.

M-16 rifles at the ready, they skirted around the exposed trap and resumed their advance to a Viet Cong encampment they knew about from a villager whose son had been healed by the medic with the squad.

Alert for enemy sentries, more traps and tripwires, the squad moved in slow stop-and-start movements toward the forest ahead. Checking the ground ahead before each step, they ignored the urge to swat the mosquitoes that bit their faces, necks and hands.

They followed the trail into the cooler shade of trees and dense foliage. The jungle was deathly quiet. Thirty yards later they crouched in the brush at the edge of a grassy clearing, about twenty yards across.

The officer, a recent West Point and Ranger school graduate, knelt next to The Virginian. In silence their eyes probed the other side of the clearing, bush-by-bush, for enemy presence. A minute of tense silence passed, then another.

Deciding it was safe to cross, the officer started to stand when someone seized him by his web belt from behind and pulled him back down. He turned his head to discover it was the medic gripping his belt and shaking his head.

"What the—"

"VC ambush in the brush at one o'clock, sir," the medic whispered.

The officer took his time peering again through the brush at the dense foliage across the clearing. "I don't see anything," he muttered. He turned toward The Virginian and lifted his chin, questioning.

"We doan' nevuhr go on patrol without Doc, suhr. If he says an ambush is ahaid, it's theah," he verified, whispering.

The officer snorted in disbelief. He had yet to taste combat and was eager for his first fight. He started to stand again.

The medic yanked the officer to the ground by his web belt a second time. Without saying a word, he pulled the pin of a grenade and lobbed it across the clearing into the center of the suspected brush. The screams of men and the familiar rattle of AK-47s on automatic fire erupted when it exploded.

The soldiers hugged the ground as bullets whizzed wildly around and above them, indicating they had caught the enemy napping. At the officer's order the Americans raked the brush where the enemy fire came from with automatic rifle fire. In a few seconds, enemy gunfire ceased.

The squad crossed the clearing at a steady walk, shoulder-to-shoulder, laying down a shield of blistering fire from M-16 rifles and an M-60 machine gun, the bullets cutting down brush and grass like so many scythes, exposing and killing the remaining guerillas.

As soon as the firefight ended, the medic began treating their only casualty–a soldier with a minor leg wound. The officer approached the medic, pure astonishment on his face.

"How did you know?" he asked. The medic kept his eyes on treating his fellow soldier's wound.

Without looking at the officer, the medic replied, "I

have advance knowledge of danger—like a sixth sense, sir."

"Well, Hitchcock, you saved my life twice today and I am at a loss as to how to thank you."

"You're welcome, sir," Hitchcock replied, never taking his attention from his patient.

The officer turned to leave, then stopped. "One more thing: Your flight to Fort Lewis for discharge is in a week. According to the men, when you're with them on patrols, all the dying is on the other side. I'd be grateful if you'd extend for another year with us. A healthy pay bonus would be arranged."

Hitchcock finished bandaging the solider and looked up at the officer. "Thank you, sir, but after two years here, it's time to go home."

"What will you do—return to boxing?"

"No, sir. I'll be picking pick up where I left off. Pre-med, sir."

The officer chuckled and nodded. "A boxer who's also a medical student. A rare combination if I ever saw one."

The soldiers moved fast, backtracking from the enemy dead to a hastily abandoned VC camp. They followed tracks from the camp to the bank of a canal of standing brown water about fifteen yards across. Dense stands of tall reeds obscured the opposite bank.

The officer looked to Hitchcock.

"They crossed here, less than twenty minutes ago,

sir," Hitchcock said, nodding at the water. "The darker water is bottom muck they stirred up when they waded to the other side. They'll have posted a rear guard in those reeds in case we try to follow them."

"Should we go in after them?" the officer asked, deferring to Hitchcock's supernatural ability.

"The tracks are mostly children's, which means mothers are with them, sir. We probably killed most if not all of the men, which leaves the mothers to do rear guard duty."

The silence between them stretched out as the officer studied the water and beyond.

"Another thing, sir. The water in the middle is chest deep."

"Um-hm," the officer muttered as he studied the width of the canal and the reeds, which were tall and dense enough to conceal several men. "We'd be wiped out in seconds in open water, and snakes would get the rest of us," he muttered. "Killing women and children is what the enemy does. Not us. Back to camp."

THE OFFICER TOOK advantage of Hitchcock's remaining time, pursuing leads daily from the Vietnamese Hitchcock treated for injuries and diseases. In every instance, the search and destroy missions ended as The Virginian said, "the enemy did all the dying."

Stateside
Two Weeks Later

WAR PROTESTORS HOLDING signs fell silent and couldn't look the dozen uniformed soldiers their own age in the eyes as they deplaned at the San Francisco airport.

A shaggy-haired youth wearing a peace symbol dangling on a leather thong around his neck blocked Hitchcock as he hurried to catch his connecting flight to Seattle. "Wish you'd died there, baby-killer," he said as he spat on Hitchcock's uniform.

Without saying a word or setting his duffel bag down, Hitchcock dropped him with one punch to the jaw as he hurried to catch his plane.

During the flight to Seattle, Hitchcock struggled to digest the glimpse of societal changes he had seen for the first time.

At the Seattle airport, he was again dismayed to see a small group of dancing, chanting young men and women, imitating the appearance of Buddhist monks, shaved heads, flowing long orange chiffon robes, pestering travelers for money and handing out tracts.

"Who–or what, are they?" he asked a man walking next to him.

"They call themselves Hare-Krishnas. Some sort of weird hippie brainwash movement," the man scoffed.

One of the Krishnas Hitchcock recognized as a high school classmate, an honor roll student, voted by their class as "most likely to succeed." The former classmate suddenly recognized Hitchcock and walked steadily toward him, orange robe flowing, sandals, flowers in hand, smiling, a glazed look on his face.

Hitchcock remembered him as the handsome, clean-cut, senior class president who gave the graduation speech four years ago. He stopped abruptly and his smile faded as he looked Hitchcock's uniform up and down and the ribbons on his chest. His gaze fell to the floor, his shoulders sagged as he turned and walked away. Troubled by what he had seen on his first day back home, Hitchcock boarded the Army bus for Fort Lewis.

The parades and welcome home parties his father received when he returned from war in 1945 didn't happen for Hitchcock. He received cold stares instead, or looks of pity, contempt, or even hatred wherever he went in uniform.

SETTLED INTO HIS mother's home a few days later, he was filling out re-enrollment papers for the UW medical school when the local news channel showed Seattle Police officers and State Patrol troopers in riot gear. Though heavily outnumbered, they held the line against mobs of war protesters who shut down rush hour traffic on the I-5 freeway in Seattle.

His mother stepped into the room. "Your friend and former neighbor, Joel Otis is here to see you," she said, smiling.

Except for his dark blue police uniform, Otis, the older brother Hitchcock never had, looked the same— tall, broad-shouldered, and charismatic. Despite his boyish facial features, he had an air about him of being in charge. His force of personality preceded him like an invisible wall. His face lit up as he greeted Hitchcock with a hearty handshake. "Welcome back, little brother."

"This is a surprise. When did you become a cop, Joel?"

"About three years ago." Otis said, flashing a grin. "Thought you might like to ride with me on patrol tonight so we can catch up."

THE SOUND OF officers being dispatched to different kinds of calls mesmerized Hitchcock as he buckled his seat belt.

He turned to Otis. "After watching the Seattle PD in action handling the riot at the federal courthouse on tv tonight, Joel, I've decided to join up with them."

"What happened to medical school?"

"I'll put it on hold for a little while," he replied. "Police work is something I want to do."

He turned his attention back to dispatchers sending officers to a parking lot disturbance, and two others to a family fight in progress. His pulse accelerated when Otis radioed that he would back up another officer who was following a stolen car. He watched as Otis flipped the console switch to activate his red overhead emergency light and accelerated through traffic.

A half-mile later Otis fell in behind the pursuing officer heading north toward the 520 freeway. The object of pursuit, a white late '60s Dodge Charger, had pulled over and stopped on the freeway onramp.

"Stay here, Roger," Otis commanded as he removed the shotgun mounted on the transmission hump of his cruiser. He leaned into the driver window and warned, "Don't do anything, no matter what happens."

A state trooper arrived behind Otis's cruiser, got out and joined Otis and the other officer.

Hitchcock couldn't see the arrest being made because of the police cruiser in front of him but he did see the other Bellevue officer place a handcuffed white male in the back of his cruiser.

Otis returned. "We're gonna stand by for the impound, while the officer we assisted takes the suspect to the station for booking," he said as he re-racked the shotgun. "By the way, I don't recommend joining Seattle PD."

"Why not?" Hitchcock asked, surprised. "Seattle's much bigger. They've got the waterfront, Skid Row, Chinatown, lots going on all the time. Bellevue's just a bedroom town."

"Not for much longer. Bellevue is where the future is," Otis replied. "It annexed all the way from Lake

Washington to Lake Sammamish while you were away. It's the fourth largest city in the state, and it will be the equivalent of Seattle in the region east of Lake Washington."

Hitchcock shifted in his seat, thinking.

"Corruption charges are about to explode in Seattle. It'll smear SPD's image for years to some," Otis added. "You don't want any part of it."

"I haven't heard or read anything about it on the news."

"It's coming, and heads are gonna roll," Otis affirmed, making Hitchcock wonder how he knew this. "They're hiring cops here like crazy because of the annexations. We're understaffed and trying to catch up. Get in on the ground floor. Use me as a reference."

Hitchcock shot a glance at Otis. "Really?"

"Well, duh, we grew up next door to each other. I taught you baseball and woods skills. That oughta count for something."

† † †

One Year Later
Tuesday, September 1970 - 6:00 P.M.

THE STREETS OF Tacoma glistened from another day of drizzly rain coming in from Puget Sound. The air stank as it always did from the pulp mills on the waterfront, a fact of life the locals derisively called "the aroma of Tacoma." As Chicago is to New York, so Tacoma is to Seattle, more industrial, more rough-and-tumble, more violent, and not a little self-conscious of its second-fiddle status.

Reflections of headlights sparkled on wet asphalt as dusk approached. Passing tires made a soft whishing sound. Mid-September meant colder nights and people going home from work to stay warm and dry instead of heading to the city parks and the waterfront.

An unusual number of police cars suddenly poured into the downtown core from different directions, often passing each other, cruising slowly, combing streets and alleys from the freeway to the docks.

ROBERT SANDOVAL SHIVERED as he hid from the police behind the dumpster of the Richfield gas station near the I-5 freeway. Wiry, medium height, in his mid-twenties, dark brown hair to his shoulders, his mustache and goatee, set against a complexion paled from incarceration, gave him a fierce, radical look, enhanced by the orange county jail jumpsuit he wore.

A gray-haired man parked a maroon late model Buick LeSabre by the restrooms and leave the driver door open as he dashed to the exterior men's restroom.

Seeing no one else around, Sandoval sprinted to the restroom and slammed the door. He came out minutes later, wearing the older man's clothes. After he had driven a block, he cursed when he saw the gas gauge read empty.

Heart pounding, he cruised the waterfront at slow

speed, his heart pounding, glancing left and right, trying to figure a way out of Tacoma before the fuel ran out. Cops were everywhere. The strongarm robbery of the old man and theft of his car would be discovered and broadcast by the police any minute, if it hadn't already.

Sandoval started to panic when a Tacoma Police car slowly passed him going the opposite direction. He ducked into the back lot of a closed garage, watching and hoping the cop would keep going. He breathed a sigh of relief when the cruiser's brake lights came on as it turned onto a side street.

Fearing the cop would return, Robert ditched the stolen Buick among other cars behind the garage. Hiding behind an old tow-truck bearing the name of the shop, he noticed a white, new Triumph TR6 two cars from his position. He eased the door open, and felt Lady Luck's smile when he discovered a key above the visor. He turned the key in the ignition. Another smile from Lady Luck — a full gas tank!

TWENTY-SIX MILES north of Tacoma, across Lake Washington from Seattle, in a second-floor apartment in the Eastgate area of Bellevue, Troy Murdoch awoke after sleeping all day. His head and body ached from the cocaine high of the night before. He yawned and scratched his scrawny arms as he emptied his last can of beef chili into a pan and turned the stove on.

He went to answer a knock at the door. "Bob! I

thought you were in jail in Tacoma!"

"Just got out today," Sandoval replied with a cryptic grin. His eyes scanned the apartment as he shouldered Troy aside. "The Army couldn't hold me, neither could the law. They're all over Tacoma looking for me, so I came up here. Mitch around?"

"Uh, h-he'll be back soon. W-well, uh, h-how long will you be around here, uh, Bob?" Troy asked, his hands dangling at his sides, twitching.

Robert shrugged as he noticed a brick on the coffee table. "What's with the brick? Got any coke?"

"Uh, w-wish I did, man," Troy gulped. "Used up what I had last night. Got wasted," he said with a timid smile.

Robert kept staring at Troy as he pointed at the brick.

Shoved his hands into his jeans pockets so Robert wouldn't see them trembling, Troy replied "The brick— uh, we g-got it for the b-barbecue outside. One of the legs b-b-broke off."

Robert took the pan off the stove, and picked up a spoon from the sink. "Where we can get more coke?" he asked between swallows of chili.

"Uh, the restaurant down the hill, a-along the freeway. The w-woman there, uh, s-s-sells only t-to those who sell," Troy stammered. Sh-she knows me, but I'm broke. Save some chili for me, Bob. That's my last can."

Robert licked the spoon as he stared at Troy, noticing his trembling.

"Say please."

"Please, Bob."

"Please Bob what, Troy?"

Troy gulped. "P-please Bob, give me my chili."

Robert shoveled the last spoonful into his mouth and tossed the empty pan in the sink. "Too late, Troy."

He held up a wad of bills from his latest victim's wallet. "Are we in business to go to the woman at the restaurant now?"

MITCH THOMAS ARRIVED at the apartment two hours later, a half-rack of beer under his arm. The sight of Troy and Bob Sandoval on the couch, each with a straw, snorting lines of white powder on a mirror on the coffee table alarmed him. He knew they were high from a few seconds of watching them ramble excitedly, slurring words in incomplete sentences about motor-cycles, fist-fights, and the women of the old days at The Spanish Castle and Parker's Ballroom.

The evil momentum of the scene was building and it frightened Mitch. He wanted to escape, for he knew what was coming, but he couldn't leave Troy.

Robert stared at Mitch, saying nothing. Holding his fear of Robert in check, Mitch joined in the snorting of cocaine until Troy got Robert to tell how he escaped from jail and came to Bellevue in a hot car.

Hearing this, Mitch switched to beer and kept a nervous eye on Robert, who swiftly became sullen and morose.

"I want Paige!" Robert exploded so suddenly the walls seemed to shake. "Where is she?"

"We got no clue where Paige is these days, Bob," Mitch said, his voice quivering.

"Maybe she's back in jail," Troy said, slurring his words.

Robert, leaning forward on the couch, wagged his head emphatically, making his greasy locks whip his face side to side. "She ain't in jail," his voice rumbled. "She's here somewhere. You guys better tell me." His head lifted but not his eyes. Eyelids lowered like hoods, snake-eyes staring at the coffee table, brooding, oozing menace.

Mitch's delicate hand shook as he reached for his beer. He looked at Robert. "That your TR6 out there?"

Robert grunted and muttered unintelligible words as he watched himself fold his fingers into scarred, calloused fists, then unfold them, repeating the process over and over, working terror into the two other hearts in the room.

"Is it fast, Bob?" Mitch asked, desperate to divert what he knew was coming.

Robert hung his head, staring at the floor, brooding.

"Y-yeah, Mitch, B-Bob t-took me out in it today," Troy volunteered.

"Yeah? And?" Mitch said, desperate to draw Robert into the conversation before he exploded.

"Cool, M-Mitch, cool. You sh-should ask Bob for a r-ride, Mitch," Troy stuttered, unable to quell the panic building inside him.

"Where's Paige, Mitch?" Robert demanded, coming out of his sullen silence.

Mitch swallowed hard. "Uh, well, I hear she got married, Bob. Got a baby."

Robert covered his face with his hands and after a moment descended into a frenzy of sobbing and moaning. He began pacing the room, crying and cursing in guttural tones, scaring his hosts into a terrified silence.

"So!" Robert shouted, choking with emotion, "Paige is gonna give *my* baby—*our* baby, to some rotten scumbag? Not my kid! No way in hell!"

He aimed his finger and thumb at Troy, simulating a gun. "Tell me who he is!"

Troy had seen Robert like this before. He wasn't so high on cocaine that he couldn't recognize a deteriorating, dangerous situation. He couldn't control the shaking in his hands. "N-never m-met him, B-Bob, n-never knew the guy's n-name. You got-gotta believe me, please, B-Bob," he slurred, his tone pleading.

Robert leaned forward from the waist, his greasy hair partly covering his glaring eyes, holding a bottle of beer in one hand. He stood over Troy, sitting on the couch.

"I. Know. You. Know. Where. They. Are, Troy," he snarled. "Tell me! I wanna get Paige and my baby. You don't, I'll—"

"Troy's telling the truth, Bob. Word on the street is they're in Seattle. Somewhere on Capitol Hill." Mitch offered, anxiously rocking his slender frame back and forth, clutching his knees with both hands.

Robert chugged down the last of his beer and let out a loud belch. The bottle exploded when he hurled it across the room, causing Mitch and Troy to exchange terrified glances, speechless and paralyzed. Robert approached Mitch, shaking his head threateningly and pointed at Troy. "Take me to Paige and my baby, Mitch—or Troy dies."

"Y-you-you can't kill Troy, Bob!"

"Can't I?" Robert snorted. "That's my *baby*! No one else's," he hissed, clenching his teeth so hard his jowls shook. He pulled a car key from his pocket. Mitch snatched it from him.

"I can't let you drive like this, Bob! We'll all go back to prison!" Mitch cried.

"If I can't find Paige tonight...I'm gonna kill a lotta people, then *I'll* die..."

"Bob, let her go, man! Paige is married. She's got another kid on the way. You're on the run and we're on parole!" Mitch pleaded.

Robert stood, glaring into space, seething, clenching

his fists.

"Bob, let it go!" Mitch begged, his voice shaking. "Move on with your life!"

Troy and Mitch exchanged nervous glances as Robert lowered his head, covered his face with his hands and broke into tears.

Robert's wailing stopped abruptly after a few seconds. He picked up the brick on the coffee table. He stepped closer to Troy and raised the hand that held the brick.

"Bob, no!" Mitch shouted.

CHAPTER ONE
The Night of the TR6

Bellevue Police Station
Tuesday, September 1970 - 8:00 P.M.

A SUDDEN FOREKNOWLEDGE of murder interrupted Hitchcock's inspection of his patrol car. He nudged the butt of his service revolver, a blued Smith & Wesson Model 10 Military & Police, four-inch bull barrel, in .38 Special with his elbow as he paused to assess it. The night air felt calm and cool and smacked of rain.

After twelve months of riding with Ira Walker, his Field Training Officer, tonight and the following night would complete his first week on patrol by himself. Every shift had been quiet so far, and he wanted it to stay that way.

The foreboding waxed stronger as he resumed checking lights, signals, siren, fluid and fuel levels, under the front and back seats for contraband that a prisoner might have ditched. Everything, including the emergency gear in the trunk, checked out.

He removed one last item for inspection, the street cop's heavy artillery, the Remington 870 twelve-gauge pump shotgun, a close-range dreadnought in an officer's hands. It was kept ready for action, mounted upright in an electronic locking rack on the transmission hump, barrel down, wooden butt stock pointed upward.

He ensured the weapon was "cruiser ready," chamber empty, four rounds of 00 buckshot in the magazine tube under the barrel. Nine .33 caliber balls in each round, capable at close range of vaporizing flesh and bone, penetrating barricades, even stopping a car by shattering its engine block.

His inspection finished, Hitchcock stepped back to admire his cruiser, a gleaming new black-and-white 1970 Plymouth Fury which emanated order and authority. Its 383 cubic-inch V8 factory-modified engine, enhanced cooling system, heavy duty brakes, racecar suspension, rubber mat floors and roll bars rivaled Ford's Police Interceptor package.

The City's service shop added the wire mesh screen between front and back seats for officer safety, front bumper push-bars, a center console for writing and holding papers, and a roof-mounted emergency-light officers called a bubble-gum machine.

Forgetting about the premonition of homicide for

the moment, he listened to units responding to calls all around the city, all were low-key in nature. The radio traffic was music to his ears as he inspected himself in the reflection of the driver door window. His dark blue uniform was fresh from the cleaners, and he liked how he looked in it.

Other squad members rolled out of the station and radioed in service while he waited for Ira Walker. His former partner for a year was explaining to Sergeant Breen why he came in on his night off, in uniform. He shook a Winston from the pack in his shirt pocket and lit it, careful to not drop ashes on his clean uniform.

Minutes later, Walker trudged out of the station toward Hitchcock's cruiser, burden visible in every step. "Come on, crime fighter—while we're young! The bad guys are waitin' for us."

Walker opened the door. His heft caused the seat to shift as he settled in.

"So, what's the latest on the home front?"

Walker snorted. "Donna found out our next cost-of-living increase will be retroactive."

"Uh-oh," was Hitchcock's contribution.

"Uh-oh is right. Her attorney is already jacking me up for more bucks. As it is, she's getting the house, child support, *and* maintenance. I'm so broke I can't pay attention. I'm living in the basement of my own home while she's dating a guy in front of me and my kids."

"Ouch. Remind me to never get married."

Walker stared solemnly ahead as Hitchcock put the car in gear. "Roger, stay single."

"I didn't mean *right now*, Ira. Try thinking ahead."

"I *am* thinking ahead. We haven't left the station yet, have we? What if you fall in love again tonight? You found a new 'this is *the* one' on the job almost every week for the year I was your training officer. I kept crossing my fingers and praying the rosary that you weren't blowing your pay on engagement rings! On the other hand, watching you with the ladies was so entertaining I sold my TV."

Hitchcock chuckled and shook his head. "I give up. Let's catch some bad guys."

"Nope, nope, nope," Walker said, shaking his head. "I came in on my night off for a few hours of tranquility–a little shooting the breeze, maybe you buy me a good meal and handle any work that comes our way. I'm your *guest* tonight. Remember that–G-U-E-S-T. Your probation ended last week. You're one of us now so relax. No hot-dog stuff. Besides, tonight should be quiet."

"Sure, Tuesdays usually are quiet, Ira, but this is gonna be a Code Three night. Somebody's gonna die on our watch."

Walker grinned patiently as an adult would to a kid. "Okay. If you say so–*Swami*!" he chuckled.

NEITHER MAN SPOKE as they cruised in and out of

patches of silvery moonlight and dark shadows along the dark, tree-lined curves of Richards Road on their way to Eastgate. They didn't need talk to communicate. A year of handling calls together resulted in a bond of unspoken trust in which each knew what to expect of the other in any situation.

The duo had much in common—but not physically.

Before the Army, Walker's strength and frame enabled him to become state champion heavyweight wrestler in high school and college. His hulking Neanderthal presence resembled the cartoon caveman Alley Oop. His brute power in overcoming resistors to arrest made him a locker room legend on the Department.

Hitchcock, by contrast, looked like Tarzan in a police uniform. The former Golden Gloves heavyweight boxer radiated a gentle, friendly manliness the public liked; women especially. Even undesirable types recognized he was *for* them, not out to nail them for anything he could.

"Good thing you're so comfortable in District Six, Roger," Walker said, breaking the silence. "Because the Brass plans on letting you languish here. To them, Eastgate is so dead you won't get into trouble. They think you need time to mellow a bit, so they're leaving you in Siberia."

"Fine by me," Hitchcock said, keeping his eyes on the road "Eastgate is my choice over any other district.

The criminals are hard-working, serious crooks—real bad guys, not spoiled juveniles, or hippie trash wearing the flag on the seat of their pants, or communist radicals spewing hate, robbing banks or kidnapping rich people's kids. I'll take honest, redneck crooks any day."

"Your understanding of Eastgate is right on," Walker said, "but the Brass remains stuck in the past. Even after a home-grown crime syndicate converted the old Sunset Drive-In into The Bavarian Gardens, a topless bar, they think nothing's going on."

"That happened while I was away," Hitchcock said.

"Knowing your weakness for women, I bet you went there often when it was a drive-in theater, huh?"

"No comment," Hitchcock said, grinning.

Walker nodded in a knowing manner. "I was here when it happened," he said. "Within weeks, brothels disguised as massage parlors sprang up close by, providing after-hours work for exotic dancers, full time prostitutes, pimps, drug dealers and straying husbands, who often drifted into the bars and no-tell-motels of next door Eastgate."

"Like Charlie's and the two motels across the driveway?"

"Changing the subject, Roger, here's a heads-up. One review board member was dead-set on failing you at the end of your probation."

"What? Who was it?"

"Lieutenant Bostwick. He stormed out when our

votes in your favor to pass you overruled his and we wouldn't change them. He wanted you gone."

"What did I ever do to him? We've never said three words to each other."

Walker shrugged. "Both sergeants asked him why, but he wouldn't answer. When he didn't return to the meeting, we passed you by unanimous vote. You're in. You have Civil Service protection now, but watch your back around Bostwick."

"Noted."

WITH NO CALLS holding, Hitchcock and Walker followed their usual routine of checking the industrial area below the freeway: closed buildings, equipment yards and vehicles. They shook doors, and tested windows in synch with each other without speech, in and out of their patrol car, leaving a window down in case a call came in. Walker taught Hitchcock to do this at the start of his shift so he could detect any changes when he repeated the process later in his shift if time allowed. In past times the procedure had resulted in catching burglars and saboteurs red-handed.

They checked the local bars next, starting at Charlie's Place, a neighborhood tavern on the north frontage road, a blue collar, pull-tab, pool table-and-beer type joint with a well-earned reputation for fights. Mechanics, road crew workers, gas pump jockeys, welders and machinists from Boeing and the Kenworth truck plant, and construction men made up its clientele.

Twin '40s vintage bungalow motels across the driveway, and Art's Burger Bar next door to Charlie's Place made Eastgate home-away-from-home for long-haul truckers, and place for local, part-time hookers and straying spouses to do business.

On paydays, local single women, most of them divorced moms, gussied up in order to moonlight at Charlie's in the world's oldest profession to make ends meet. The revenue the part-time ladies of the night brought in helped put food on their tables, shoes on their kids, and kept the motels afloat in hard times. They could still pay their employees, taxes, and keep the lights on.

THEY PARKED IN the shadows at the far edge of the parking lot of Charlie's Place by a gravel pit, among silent bulldozers, their engine and lights off, windows rolled down a couple inches for better hearing. From here they had a commanding view of the back of Charlie's Place and the two motels. In silence they watched and listened, absorbing and assessing the environment.

"The crowd'll be thin tonight because tomorrow is payday," Hitchcock commented.

They adjusted their hats, slipped their batons into their belt rings and strolled through the parking lot, probing inside the dozen cars and trucks with their flashlights, checking for drug dealers and users, finding none.

Hitchcock opened the rear door of Charlie's a crack to listen. They heard Merle Haggard singing *"I'm an Okie From Muskogee"* on the jukebox. Calm chattering, laughter, and clinking pool balls dropping into table pockets blended with musty odors of cigarette smoke, beer and deep-fried food. Satisfied they wouldn't be walking into a fight or a robbery, they ambled in as the amiable neighborhood cops they were, smiling and greeting people by name.

The owner, mountainous Wallace Evans, greeted them from behind the bar. "Hey, Roger, how are 'ya?" His huge hands rested on the scarred walnut counter, smiling, shirt cuffs rolled up, exposing thick, hairy wrists.

Hitchcock appreciated that Evans liked having the bluesuits walk through unexpectedly every night. To him the cops' visits made his rowdy bar a safer place, kept a lid on things. A family man who wanted people to call him Wally, Evans possessed a playful sense of humor and an endless repertoire of clean jokes. But tonight, Hitchcock sensed something had Wally rattled.

"So, what's up, friend?"

"I was just about to call you," Wally said in a confidential tone below the music, "and here you are."

Hitchcock grinned. "No present like the time."

"A strange guy left a few minutes ago. Had the look

and way about him of having done hard time. His appearance and the way he moved creeped me out. In fact, I'm still jumpy."

Hitchcock looked intently at Evans, knowing him to be able to read people like newsprint. "Tell me more, big man."

Wally set his meaty hands palms-down on the bar and shook his head in dismay as he stared Hitchcock in the eyes. "He came in alone, ordered a beer, sat at the corner table over there, watching me and my customers for about thirty minutes."

"What else did he do?"

Wally shrugged "Just sat there, stone-faced."

"That's it?" Hitchcock asked, puzzled.

Wally's stare at Hitchcock hardened. "This is a nice, friendly neighbor-hood bar," he said. "Sure, it gets a little rowdy once in a while, but it's pretty much the same crowd all the time. Strangers come here some, but never do they make me nervous. But this guy got my hackles up right away. I think he was casing my place."

"Description?"

"White guy, thirty-five or so, real pale skin, thin build, but fit, like a soldier or a martial arts type. Five nine or ten, short brown hair, average features. Had the look about him of having done prison time–soulless eyes."

"Any facial hair, scars or tattoos?" Walker asked.

Wally shook his head. "Clean shaven. No marks

that I saw."

"Do you remember anything he said?"

"He spoke almost in a whisper to order a beer," Wally replied. "Later when I asked him if he wanted another, he shook his head. Didn't say anything else."

Wally paused for a moment. He picked up a towel and rubbed the bar surface with it, looking down, his brows knit together in a furrow. "Could you guys be here when I close at midnight and follow me home?"

"Sure. I'll tell our sergeant, so if we can't be here, another unit will show up. We're gonna check around, see if we can find him. Be back later," Hitchcock said.

They split up to talk to the night clerks at The Eastgate and Kane's, twin motels. Both said they hadn't seen anyone matching Wally's description. Because of the popularity of police scanners with the public, Hitchcock called Sergeant Breen from a pay phone to advise him of Wally's information and request for an escort at midnight if he and Walker were on another detail.

A FEW BLOCKS down the two-lane Highway 10 frontage road from Charlie's Place, sandwiched between a tool rental shop and a mom-and-pop insurance agency in a vintage flat-roofed one-story brick building of early 1950s vintage, was The Great Wall, a hole-in-the wall Chinese joint.

Its dining area consisted of a dozen small wooden

tables that could be pushed together to accommodate parties of more than four customers. Locals ate at the restaurant but avoided the forbidding aura of the small, dark cocktail lounge in the back Conversely, Orientals from Seattle drank in the bar but avoided the food.

Daytime, The Great Wall came across as just another small Chinese lunch and dinner joint with a bar in the back. But after adjacent businesses closed, the place drew night creatures–rats, bats and alley cats–animal and human. Local folklore had it that those who tried to penetrate its secrets or became involved with its mysterious owner either disappeared or came to ruin.

Hitchcock nestled their black-and-white cruiser in the dirt lot behind The Great Wall among road graders, bulldozers, and dump trucks belonging to Lakeside Sand-and-Gravel. From here, with windows down, they could see past the open kitchen door. The clear night air carried conversation in the kitchen to them as if they were only feet apart. None of it was in English.

After a few minutes they walked past the owner's new black Cadillac El Dorado into deafening clouds of pungent steam gushing upward from two over-sized wok pans. Heaps of raw meat and vegetables hissed and sizzled, droplets of hot grease popped and flew in all directions.

A squat, heavy, broad-faced Asian woman with meaty hands, a greasy white apron over her clothes, her age impossible to guess, stood at the stainless-steel prep table with a paring knife, cutting and stripping hide and sinew from four deer legs—hair and hooves still intact. She didn't look up as she tossed chunks of tendon into a wok filled with raw vegetables and other meats of questionable origin. Around her, the cook, waitresses and food preppers barked rapid-fire orders at each other in their native tongue as they scurried around, ignoring the cops.

Hitchcock's jaw fell open. He leaned toward Walker and whispered, "Deer legs? How do they bill *that* on the menu? As this week's roadkill special? Wouldn't the Health Department love to know about *this*?!"

Walker snickered. He covered his mouth as he said, "it's got a name, but it ain't on the menu."

Hitchcock's eyes widened. "What?"

"Mystery meat," Walker whispered with a smirk and a nudge of his elbow.

A sultry female voice with a foreign accent purred behind them. "Hullo, po-leese mans. Can I get you boys something? Some coffee, maybe, or tea? Tea I got ready."

The owner, Juju Kwan, a luscious, exotic beauty from Taiwan, in her early thirties, who could pass for much younger, came up alongside Hitchcock. When he looked down at her, she stepped in front of him, offering him a better view of herself. A filmy, sleeveless black dress, low-cut and form-fitting, flowed over her hourglass shape. Lustrous black hair draped over her ivory shoulders like fine silk, framing her perfect, aquiline facial features. The bow shape of her full lips intensified her already strong sensuality. Her large almond-shaped brown eyes flashed invitingly up at Hitchcock as she put a delicate hand on his arm, squeezing his bicep.

"Ooh, you strong man, Heetchcock," Juju said with a subtle shake of her head. "You famous boxer, yes?" she said, smiling and holding up her other hand clenched into a fist. "You come see me sometime, yes? I take good care of you." Her voice radiated lust and seduction.

Hitchcock couldn't help looking down into Juju's jaw-dropping beauty. Of the rarest order, she was, the kind that turns boys into men, and men into boys, who can cast seductive spells on men, no matter how many times they had seen her before.

She reminded Hitchcock of the *mama-sans*, the boss women who ran bars and brothels in Southeast Asia, where prostitutes were often slaves–young, poor, and destined to be sold or left to starve once they became diseased or too old for men's tastes.

From his military years in Southeast Asia, he knew that beneath Juju's come-here-boy-me-like-you façade, lurked a cruel, cunning tigress, who prided herself on her ability to lure naive, sheltered local men into leaving their homes for her just because she could. He had heard rumors that one or two local women *paid* Juju to leave their husbands alone in order to save their marriages and homes.

"Nothing for us, thanks." Hitchcock replied with a polite smile. "We're looking for a potentially dangerous man who may have come here tonight. We'll have a quick look around and be out of here, okay?"

"Oh sure, Heetchcock. You go ahead, you check, but be careful please, *for me*, please, but tell me—what he look like?" Juju asked, looking at him, keeping her hand on his arm.

He repeated Wally's description without mentioning Wally.

"No. No one come here like that," Juju said, gesturing with her other hand toward the dark recesses of her cocktail lounge. "Please, check my bar. If he here, you arrest him! I run clean shop here. No bad men, only good people here."

Hitchcock and Walker gave the bar a quick look-through. Only three well-dressed Asian men were present.

Walker began laughing as they settled into their cruiser.

"What's so funny?"

"You—your face when we walked in," Walker said, still laughing. "Us older guys have been telling you, *never* eat there. The employees don't speak English, probably because they were smuggled here on ships. Where they come from, they eat whatever meat their hands find. The look on your face when you saw deer legs being tossed into the wok was priceless."

"I thought about calling the health department."

"Not for long, you didn't," Walker chuckled. "Juju moved in *between* you and the deer feet. She placed her tiny hand on your arm, started squeezing and flashed those big browns up at you and you went 'huh? What deer legs?' With one touch she wrapped you around her little finger."

Hitchcock, always one to laugh at himself, chuckled with Walker. "Juju's beautiful, but I wouldn't trust her as far as I could throw her. I admit she distracted me," he said. "How not—just look at her. So, the laugh's on me."

"She knows you don't like her," Walker said. "But because Juju is what she is, and you're a cop, she thinks you'll be another notch on her belt sooner or later. So, I hope you *got it* because you have a weakness for women—and they for you."

"Guilty as charged."

"Remember the three B's I told you will bring down a cop every time."

"Booze, broads, and bucks," they recited together.

NO ONE THEY talked to at the other bars and motels had seen the man Wally described. "Looks like Wally's getting a bit jumpy in his old age," Walker said meditatively as they walked back to their cruiser.

"I'm not so sure," Hitchcock said. "Wally's been in

the bar business too many years to not have people-savvy."

"Yeah, well, I'm hungry, and it's ten now, so the joints here are closed. I'll ask if we can leave our district to eat."

Walker keyed the mic. "Three Zero Six to Radio, request permission to leave our district to 10-34 at Sambo's."

"Permission granted, Three Zero Six."

Hitchcock headed toward the freeway when Dispatch came on the air. *"All units standby. Emergency traffic only."*

Hitchcock heard urgency in the dispatcher's voice: *"Three Zero Six, return to your district. Three Zero Eight, start moving to the area of the community college. Both units stand by—we're getting more information."*

Anxiety came over him as he U-turned and headed toward the college. Dispatch came on the air again: *"All units stand by. Emergency traffic only."*

He pulled into the nearest parking lot and waited. A heavy expectation came, like the air during a break in the monsoon rains of Southeast Asia at night. He glanced at Walker but said nothing. For a few seconds he relived jungle night patrols, crouching, helpless, praying the incoming shells from the artillery of the North Vietnamese Army would whoosh by and miss everyone, not knowing if his next move would be to patch up his fellow soldiers or kill the enemy, wondering who will die or lose a limb.

Anxiety filled Walker too. In the waiting he began to fidget. To do something–anything–he lit a cigarette.

Finally, *"Radio to Three Zero Six and Three Zero Eight, respond Code Three to a fight-in-progress. One male adult is unconscious from head injuries at the Ridge Apartments at 2931 145th Avenue SE, unit unknown on the second floor. The caller is also injured. Getting more details."*

Hitchcock had been there before on loud party, disturbance and underage drinking calls. He flipped the console switch for the overhead red light and headed in the direction of the call.

"Three Zero Six en route," Walker acknowledged.

"Radio to responding units. Victim on the phone says the suspect is a Bob Sandoval, white male, mid-twenties, medium build, has been taking cocaine and alcohol. He escaped from the Tacoma jail today. Says he is going to commit suicide with his car and take as many people with him as he can. Sandoval struck the other roommate on the head with a brick when he tried to take his keys."

Before either unit could acknowledge, Dispatch added: *"Caller reports the suspect left the apartment, driving a new, white Triumph TR-6, unknown license."*

Officer Jason Allard came on the air. *"Three Zero Eight arriving at the Ridge Apartments. A white TR6 is leaving the parking lot. Washington plate Adam Queen Boy Seven Two Six, heading northbound on 148th. He is not stopping."*

Hitchcock turned right, accelerating south on two-lane 145th Avenue, fast approaching the rear of a station wagon. He flipped the siren switch and hit the horn ring. *Aaaaahhhh,uuuhhhh,aahhhh.*

"Pull over, dammit!" Walker shouted, bracing his feet against the floor, his left hand gripping the wood stock of the shotgun, expecting a crash as the distance rapidly closed.

Instead of pulling over, the station wagon stopped in the southbound lane. Hitchcock hit the siren again and swerved into the oncoming lane, blazing past the station wagon with inches to spare.

"Idiot!" Walker shouted as they whizzed past.

Allard came on the air again. *"Suspect turning left on SE 22nd Street, heading to 145th."*

"We're on 145th, and we see you, Three Zero Eight," Walker radioed as Hitchcock U-turned and resumed acceleration, passing the station wagon again going the other way. He hung a hard right at the first side street, pushing hard to catch up to Allard.

Hitchcock and Allard—another Vietnam vet— chased the TR6 up and down a grid of intersecting two-lane side streets on either side of 148th Avenue, a four-lane thoroughfare, zipping around moving traffic, clocking speeds of 60, 70, 80 miles per hour.

The TR6 spun out as it attempted to make a ninety-degree right turn at an intersection. Allard tried to ram it and missed by inches. The chase resumed southbound toward the freeway on 148th Avenue, a divided four-lane thoroughfare.

Dispatch broke in: *"Both units: Suspect Sandoval has a confirmed outstanding felony warrant for Assault First Degree, Attempted Murder, out of Pierce County. The vehicle he's driving was stolen in Tacoma today. Consider Sandoval armed and dangerous."*

The chase sped south on 148th toward the freeway at over 80 miles per hour. Past the college entrance at SE 24th, 148th Avenue dropped bumpily downhill to a forced right turn onto the north frontage road which ran parallel to the westbound freeway lanes. For five blocks, only a shallow ditch separated the frontage road from the westbound lanes of Highway 10.

The TR6 barely made the right turn. Sparks flew like an armload of Fourth of July sparklers as its entire left side scraped along the concrete barrier between the end of 148th Avenue and the freeway. Careening off the barrier and accelerating west on the two-lane frontage road, the TR6 blasted past Charlie's Place, the two no-tell motels, then The Great Wall.

Allard hung hard on its heels, Hitchcock close behind, unshakeable, like two snarling sheepdogs closing in on a fleeing wolf, engines roaring, red lights flashing, sirens howling in full effect.

At seventy the TR6 zipped across the short, level onramp leaving the frontage road, entering westbound Highway 10. It accelerated downhill, headed for the East Channel Bridge then Mercer Island, the Floating Bridge, ending at Seattle.

Allard missed the onramp. Hitchcock crossed it and resumed the pursuit.

Allard leaped the ditch at seventy in an effort to stay in the chase. His left front wheel struck the shoulder of the ditch and snapped off. His cruiser slid sideways on its fender across the highway's westbound lanes, spraying sparks and smoke, presenting itself broadside in front of Hitchcock.

"Damn you, Allard!" Walker shouted, bracing his feet on the floor, gripping the shotgun stock even tighter.

Hitchcock spun out of control when he braked and veered hard right, almost colliding with Allard. Fighting panic, he let off the gas and veered hard left to avoid crashing through the guardrail. He came out of the spin, made two lesser corrections at lower speed and ended up facing west, staring at the fast-disappearing taillights of the TR6 on an otherwise empty highway.

He floored the pedal. The mighty 383 cubic inch V8 roared. The gap began to close, leaving Allard behind. Walker stared straight ahead, mute, transfixed, left hand continuing to grip the wood stock of the shotgun.

Rain pelted the windshield. Wind resistance streaked the water up and away. Speed increased. Hitchcock's peripheral vision narrowed. He could see only what was right in front of him, like blasting down a black funnel. Though Walker sat next to him, he was alone, in a realm of tiny red taillights ahead and the steering wheel in his hands.

A numbing cold, a paralysis, crept into Hitchcock as the wipers shuddered across the windshield.

Another voice came on the air: *"Three Zero Five is in position at the 104th onramp."*

"Good! Sherman's a former racecar driver. Nobody outruns Tom Sherman," Walker said in a tone of new confidence.

Another voice came on the air: *"Three Zero Six, this is Sergeant Breen. What's your speed?"*

Walker glanced at the speedometer. "Uh, looks like a hundred and ten."

"All right—call it off," Breen ordered.

Hitchcock heard nothing. He dared not take his eyes off the road. Not at this speed on wet pavement. The road became an ever-tightening funnel. Only the TR6 taillights ahead existed. *At this speed we're not in contact with the pavement, only water,* he realized. *The steering wheel feels light as air. God help us—we're starting to fishtail! Hold steady. If I take my eyes off the road, we're dead!* He flicked his eyes to the rearview mirror. *Sherman's behind us, red light flashing—closing the distance fast.*

The radio crackled. The raspy smoker's voice of Sergeant Breen came on the air: *"All units are to break off the pursuit. Again, break off the pursuit! Now!"*

No one replied. The chase entered the East Channel Bridge from Bellevue to Mercer Island, beyond which the Floating Bridge crossed Lake Washington into

Seattle.

Hitchcock's hands white-knuckled the steering wheel, jaw set, eyes riveted straight ahead.

Sergeant Breen's voice began cracking as he came on the air again. *"All units break off the—"*

"Aw hell!" Walker shouted as he turned off the radio.

SERGEANT BREEN PACED nonstop in the dispatch room, listening, dreading, chain-smoking, his face bright red, his blond crew cut glistening with sweat. The radio silence meant his officers couldn't and wouldn't stop. The chase had gone on too long. It became a deadly mix of fury, adrenaline, high speeds, a desperate felon out to kill others and himself, pursued by veterans who would pursue the suspect to whatever the end would be.

Endless "what if-s" raced through Breen's mind. He envisioned a scene of dead civilians, dead officers and terrible damage. Suddenly he snapped his fingers as he pointed at the assisting dispatcher. "Quick! Call Seattle PD Dispatch. Tell them we have two units chasing an escaped felon intent on committing homicide and suicide by car in their city, crossing Mercer Island now at over a hundred."

RAIN HAMMERED HITCHCOCK'S windshield. The wind howled; the engine roared as if thrilling to the chase. Cold fear gripped him as the cruiser began fishtailing as he entered the East Channel Bridge to Mercer Island. *This is it! We're gonna die!* Numbing cold crept into his arms and legs. His heart in his throat, he turned the wheel in the direction of the slide and let off the gas rather than try to counter the swaying. To his relief the big black-and-white quickly resumed steady in-line travel. More acceleration. The TR6 taillights grew larger.

"We gotta ram it or shoot the engine before it reaches Seattle," Walker said.

The rain stopped.

AT THE SEATTLE Police precinct on Capitol Hill, the newly promoted Sergeant Milo Lewis and two units of his squad took up positions in their cruisers on the on-ramps above the freeway. Rolling down his window, Lewis heard the faint wails of distant police sirens in the east. The chase would arrive soon, bringing destruction and possible death. With his men in position, he tightened his seat belt, lit a cigarette and waited.

THE TR6 BLASTED across the East Channel Bridge from Bellevue to Mercer Island at over a hundred. It went up the first off-ramp and flew airborne past the stop sign at the crest. A full-size sedan began crossing the overpass, headed for the off-ramp as Hitchcock zipped up the off-ramp and went airborne. The sedan on the overpass went into a slide as Hitchcock and Walker sailed through the air, narrowly missing a fatal accident.

They landed in a nose-first, two-part crash on the shoulder, stalling the engine in an exploding hail of dirt and gravel where the TR6 had been seconds before it roared to life and disappeared around a bend in the freeway, narrowly missing being crushed by Hitchcock's cruiser.

Sherman flashed by Hitchcock and Walker, taking up the chase. He rounded the bend in time to catch sight of the close-set taillights zipping down the next off-ramp and disappear. Sherman downshifted and braked down the off-ramp in time to see where the TR6 had spun out while taking the hard-left turn at the bottom to go under the freeway where it stalled, facing Sherman as he arrived. Two Mercer Island patrol cars arrived, lights flashing, blocking the suspect's escape to the rear.

Sherman approached on foot, calm as ever, shotgun at the shoulder, aimed through the windshield at the driver, who struggled desperately to restart the engine. When Sandoval's eyes met Sherman's, Sherman made a show of racking a round into the chamber and flicking the safety off.

"You're under arrest! Put your hands on the dash, palms up!"

"Die with me, pig!" Sandoval screamed, his face deathly white under fluorescent lights, contorted with rage. Flipping Sherman his middle finger, he turned the ignition again. The motor whirred but failed to turn over.

The Mercer Island officers walked up to the rear of the TR6, guns drawn, as Hitchcock and Walker ran to the driver-side door. Walker jerked on the handle. Locked. Sandoval went berserk, shaking his head, beating the dashboard with his fists, mouth foaming and spraying saliva as he screamed obscenities. He turned the key again. This time the engine began to turn over. Sherman pointed his shotgun at the hood of the TR6, finger on the trigger.

"Hold your fire!" Hitchcock yelled as he swung the head of his heavy-duty aluminum eight-cell Kel-Lite flashlight completely through the driver's door window.

Sandoval ducked as bits of broken safety glass showered him. He screamed and gripped the steering wheel with both hands when Walker seized him by the front of his jacket.

In one smooth motion the former heavyweight wrestling champion pulled Sandoval through the window like a wet towel, as though his grip on the steering wheel never happened. He pinned Sandoval face-down on the pavement, arms and legs flailing in futile resistance. Hitchcock cuffed the prisoner's hands behind him. He and Walker half-walked, half-carried Sandoval to the back of their patrol car and belted him in.

Walker turned the radio back on. He had to shout over Sandoval's screams and the noise of his kicking the doors and the cruiser ceiling as he keyed the mic: "Three Zero Six, Radio, chase ended on Mercer Island. No one injured, no property damage. We're en route to Overlake ER. Sandoval in custody. Three Zero Five will stand by for the vehicle impound."

Sandoval's thrashing began rocking the cruiser before they reached the freeway.

"Pull over, Roger," Walker said. "We gotta stop him—he's kicking the windows now—he'll break the glass if we don't."

Sandoval kicked, spit, and cursed Hitchcock and Walker as they fought him out of the car to the pavement. They removed his shoes, handcuffed his feet together and applied a third set of cuffs to connect his feet to his hands behind his back. Hitchcock on one side, Walker on the other, they lifted him by his belt. After some struggling, they set him face-down on the rear seat.

Walker tried to keep Sandoval conscious by asking him questions. "How are you feeling, Bob? We're taking you to the hospital, now, Bob. Where are you now, Bob?"

Sandoval grunted after each question.

Hitchcock and Walker rolled their windows down for cold fresh air to keep Sandoval awake as they headed back to Bellevue.

Two orderlies and a young, uniformed security guard who shivered with anxiety and cold waited outside the emergency entrance. Sandoval sang softly to himself as Walker helped the orderlies lift him out of the cruiser, set him face-down on the gurney and wheel him into the crowded emergency room.

"Isn't that awfully uncomfortable for the young man?" demanded a bespectacled, slender doctor in a white coat, his red-bearded jaw jutting forth with indignation.

"Well, Doc, this guy escaped from jail in Tacoma, stole a car, then he assaulted a guy tonight," Walker tried to explain. "And he fled when we–"

"It doesn't give you the right to truss him up like a wild animal!" The doctor shouted. "Set him loose, officer!"

"But, Doc, you don't understand. I'm trying to tell you this guy is–"

The doctor's face, even his ears, flushed red. Purple veins bulged on his forehead. "Officer, I *command* you to free him. At once!" he shouted, waving his arms.

"Please listen, Doc. This man is dangerous. He's an escaped felon, and as of tonight he's facing multiple felony assault charges, so no matter what, he'll be going with us."

"Take the handcuffs off him. NOW!"

Walker complied. "We'll wait on the other side of

the curtain."

"Out-out-out!" the doctor shrieked, pointing toward the curtain.

Minutes later a woman's scream pierced the air while Hitchcock was on the phone, updating Sergeant Breen. He heard sounds of scuffling, the doctor's voice pleading, then the sounds of breaking glass. Hitchcock glanced at Walker, who smiled knowingly.

The nurse who had been with the doctor rushed out, hair disheveled, her white uniform askew. "Officers, help! He's attacking Doctor Philips. I can't stop him!"

"Sarge, I gotta go. Nurse says the prisoner's attacking the doctor."

"I heard. Take him to Harborview, Roger," Breen said.

Hitchcock and Walker charged through the white curtains to find Dr. Philips on the floor in a protective fetal position, Sandoval was dragging him through a puddle of liquid chemicals and broken glass.

As Hitchcock broke Sandoval's grip on Doctor Philips and Walker powered him to the floor, an over-zealous young security guard stepped in and over-sprayed Sandoval's face with chemical mace. The nurse and the doctor, having no previous training or exposure to such chemicals as mace and tear gas, panicked and shrieked when the burning of the skin and eye swelling set in, and breathing became difficult.

Screaming for help, they thrashed about, but

Hitchcock and Walker, who had been trained to function through the effects of gases, ignored them except to announce, "It'll pass in minutes," as they fought through restricted breathing, burning skin and eyes to regain control of Sandoval.

"Get that animal out of here! Take him to Harborview!" a trembling Doctor Philips screamed, clutching his throat, his voice hoarse. He didn't object this time when Hitchcock and Walker trussed Sandoval up the same way as before and wheeled him on a gurney to their patrol car.

With the two front windows down and the fan on at full blast, they left the hospital, hanging their heads out the windows for air.

"Damn you, Bob!" Walker shouted, wiping his eyes. "My skin is on fire, my eyes hurt and I can't breathe!"

The increased airflow from open windows at freeway speeds didn't help much. Hitchcock pulled over. He and Walker stood at the front of the cruiser, breathing and rubbing their eyes while Sandoval hummed and sang unintelligibly.

The effects of mace were so strong they stopped and got out again for more air, this time on Mercer Island. A team of orderlies met them when they reached Harborview. They fought Sandoval again when he seized one of the orderlies by the hair the second the handcuffs were removed to place him on a gurney.

On the elevator ride to the ninth-floor psych ward,

Sandoval craned his neck and snapped his teeth, as he tried to bite Walker's hand. For Walker, who came in for a quiet ride to escape his troubles for a night, enough was enough.

To prevent the orderly from seeing what he was doing, Walker laid his right hand on Sandoval's arm and covered it with his left as he pinched and twisted hunks of skin, while soothingly asking "Oh, poor Bob! Is everything okay now, Bob? You'll be fine here, Bob. You screwed up my nice peaceful night tonight, Bob, but don't worry, we'll take care of you, Bob."

Sandoval grunted "Uhhh!" with each pinch. At the ninth floor, the psyche ward the cops referred to as "the goofy garage," they helped orderlies wrestle him into a padded cell before returning to Bellevue. Hitchcock glanced at his watch. 1:30 a.m.

SAMBO'S WAS DEAD except for one customer. Hitchcock ordered ham and eggs over easy, no hash browns or toast. Walker ordered a burger and fries. Both had coffee. They ate, and topped off their meal with a smoke, numbed into silence by the night's adrenalin-charged events.

Sergeant Breen flashed his headlights at them as they walked out of Sambo's. They pulled up beside him, windows down, expecting trouble.

"You guys deserve to be the first to be told," Breen said. "The first victim in the apartment died at Overlake a half hour ago. The second victim, the one who called us, is in critical condition and is not expected to live. You guys chased–and caught–a double murderer and prevented others from happening."

Breen paused as he stared out his windshield. "Good thing your radio 'failed' and you didn't let him go. Detectives will want your reports when you get back tonight. Finish the shift, get some rest. Somebody will complain about the chase, so before they do, I'll be writing up commendations for you boys."

As Sergeant Jack Breen, always the cops' cop, drove off, Walker turned to Hitchcock.

"What gives with your prediction of a Code Three night and that somebody would die? Are you a psychic? A paranormal?"

Hitchcock shrugged. "I can't explain it, but I see coming danger and do my best to intercept."

"Psh!" Walker snorted as he cranked his window back up. "You told me ahead of time we'd have a Code Three night, and we did. You said someone would die, and someone did. Might have *two* deaths, in fact. You could save lives with a gift like that, Roger."

"I did, in 'Nam. Somehow, I always knew where the enemy was, waiting to ambush us. We got the jump on them every time, but sometimes a few guys got hit."

Dismayed, Walker shook his head. "I bet the Cong were flabbergasted."

They returned to District Six, numbed by the

letdown after a long adrenalin rush. In mutual silence they re-checked the industrial district and businesses as the last mission of their shift. It seemed strange, but all was normal, almost as if the night of death and mayhem never happened.

Hitchcock reflected on the night's action as he refueled his cruiser. It seemed an unseen hand protected him and Walker, and restored things back to normal.

Back at the station, he eye-balled his cruiser for damage. After all the hard use he put it through, except for a few nicks in the paint from flying rocks when they landed on the gravel shoulder on Mercer Island, there was no damage.

A supervisor's comment came to mind as he drove to the station: "Plymouth builds a cheap, tough car." He had to agree.

Something on the shotgun buttstock caught his eye as he gathered his gear. He reared back when he flipped on the interior light—it was the outline of Walker's hand, fingers and thumb, indented on the wood shoulder stock!

EXHAUSTION SEEPED INTO Hitchcock as he drove the half-mile from the station to his apartment. His hopes for his first week after passing probation to end quietly ended in mayhem. The premonition he'd had proved true; it had been a night of violence and death and his first week on his own had one more night to go.

Another premonition came as he entered his apartment, removed his gun belt, changed into his sweats and poured one finger of Jack Daniels. It was different from one last night, but just as definite. He shook his head as he took a sip of whiskey, the proper drink for American men, in his opinion. *Now what?*

CHAPTER TWO
Hitchcock

THE SLOSHING AND rolling of his waterbed forced him out of his sleep. Frustrated at not having enough shuteye, he tried to clear his thoughts and lie still, but it was no use. His eyes squinted in the gray daylight seeping through the curtains of his ground floor one-bedroom apartment. The clock on his nightstand read half past noon—morning for someone on night shift.

Last night's adrenalin dump was taking its toll; his head and body ached, he didn't want to get up, but he couldn't just lay in bed, wide awake. He peered into the framed black-and-white photograph on his nightstand of two smiling men and a little boy standing in front of the Pancake Corral on its opening day. He touched the face of the tallest man. *Miss you, Dad.*

I'll catch a few more winks before work tonight, he promised himself as his feet touched the floor.

Insulated from the chill by his gray sweatshirt,

matching pants and white athletic socks, he ambled into the bachelor-size kitchen. The putrid green stove, fridge, linoleum floor, and plastic countertop squeezed into a tight space did nothing for his mood.

He reheated yesterday's coffee to a rolling boil, and poured it into his Wonderful Wyoming coffee mug, the one with a cowboy waving his hat in the air, riding a bucking bronco.

Settled into the depths of his brown leather easy chair, he reviewed last night's scenes of violence, death and tragedy. The America he grew up in and went away to protect would never call servicemen "baby killers" or policemen "pigs." The country had become a nation of scofflaws, plagued with rising violent crime, social discord, and drug addiction during his absence.

What would the rock stars, celebrities and news media people who glorify drugs say about last night's carnage? Would they blame the police for the chase, or society for a young man's death and the possible death of the other young man at the apartment, both at the hands of Sandoval, a maimed life, who would be returning to prison? he wondered.

None of last night's tragedy would have happened if not for drugs, but the news media won't mention that—getting high is fashionable now. Drugs were taboo a short time ago. What changed, and where will it take his generation, his country?

Used to be that narcotics were confined to Asian

opium dens and big city slums, never in America's suburbs or small towns. Love of country prevailed. Desecrating the flag resulted in a beating, loss of reputation and social ostracism. Only cowards dodged military service.

Now, anti-war demonstrations were everywhere. Veterans and policemen are scorned. Right is wrong— wrong is right. Ordinary crime is politicized. The weakest excuses for criminal behavior are blithely accepted in the courts.

Hitchcock didn't have political or philosophical leanings, but he realized the country turned to a dark chapter during his military years.

Though raised in the church, seeing death and dying up close and doing his best to save wounded soldiers, yet losing many, blunted his belief in God. Without blaming or discarding God, he set religion and spiritual matters aside to deal with the realities he faced as an Army medic.

His life-plan had been to follow his father's and grandfather's footsteps by becoming a medical doctor, until he came home to a different country than the one he left.

His first year on the job had been colorful, arresting people he had grown up with, often for felony drug charges, and drunk driving. Overlake, the city's first hospital, opened its Emergency Room a few months ago, but Bellevue still didn't have an ambulance service.

As it had done for years, it continued to contract with Flintoff's Mortuary, fifteen miles away in Issaquah, to use their hearses for ambulance services.

Stories of accident victims freaking out when they awoke to find themselves in the back of a hearse, and conscious people frantically refusing to go anywhere in a hearse made for years of laughs for the troops and a humorous part of the Department's history.

HIS TIMEX WATCH read 1:15. *Time to go.* He slugged down the last of his coffee, slipped into a pair of well-worn blue jeans, brown square toe harness boots and his favorite wool shirt, which years of washing and wearing had resulted in baby-blanket softness. He holstered his blued, off-duty Smith & Wesson .38 snub-nose, and covered it with his black windbreaker, then touched the photo of his father again as he left, carrying his gym bag.

The crisp autumn air stimulated his hunger as he stepped outside and fired up his two-tone gold '68 Chevy El Camino.

CHACE'S PANCAKE CORRAL began business in 1952, a ranch-style, standalone building, an icon of Old Bellevue, a mom-and-pop American roadside diner, the breakfast-and-lunch kind which never changes. Open or closed, the place seemed to wave at passers-by along 104th Avenue SE, the busy four-lane road from Bellevue's downtown to Highway 10.

Bill Chace and his wife, Louise, were working owners, helped by their teenage daughters, dark-haired Ada and blonde Jane, who worked after school and weekends as waitresses and owners-in-training.

The aroma of bacon, eggs and pancakes on the grill greeted him as he walked through the two heavy wooden front doors, covered with layers of brown paint, into the waiting area.

"What'll you have, Roger—your usual, the Weight Lifter's Special, medium rare?" Ada asked.

He smiled and shook his head. "It's morning for me, Ada. Coffee, please, buckwheat pancakes and a side of bacon."

The Corral was ready to close when he headed to the register. The ever-cheerful Bill Chace, a former member of the UW rowing team, still athletically lean in his late fifties, came up to ring him out.

"Hitch, Bill said, calling out his invented nickname, "you're looking more like your dad all the time. Built like him, too. A boxer's build. You got the arms, the shoulders, you're lean, muscular, coordinated."

"We're built the same, but Dad was taller than me."

"I would've thought you'd join the Seattle Police, Hitch."

"SPD was my first choice, but they suspended hiring due to budget cuts. Bellevue's been hiring like crazy because of the annexations. I needed a job, so here I am."

"We're glad you're on the force, Hitch, but I still

hope you become a doctor, like your dad. I never knew a more gifted medical man. One time he diagnosed my condition just by looking at me."

Hitchcock inserted a toothpick between his teeth as he said, "I'd like to hear that one, Bill."

"I went to see Ted for a checkup, and before I could say why I came, your dad said, 'Bill, your blood pressure is too high, and your kidneys aren't working right.' I had my doubts, but I didn't say anything. The tests he ran confirmed he was right. Your dad saved my life! Ted's sudden passing was a terrible loss." Chace gave a reverent shake of his head.

"It hit us hard. Our mom worst of all."

"I remember when your dad got you started in boxing," Bill continued. "I asked him 'Ted, isn't Roger pretty young to be boxing?' He told me he didn't want you to be soft and sheltered like so many boys today. He wanted you to learn life through conflict—boxing, hard work, and sacrifice, as he had from his dad. As I remember, he had you training in the same Seattle club he did."

Hitchcock smiled and nodded. "Dad gave me my first pair of gloves and started my training on my ninth birthday. I still have friends from different backgrounds because of my boxing days. Army boot camp was less of a shock because of my training."

"You worked some hard labor jobs during your summers, too, as I remember."

"I did. The summer after my sophomore year I worked at the Bar-S slaughterhouse in Seattle. After my junior year I worked on a road repair crew laying concrete drain tile. The summer after high school I worked for a roofing company. We did commercial buildings and houses."

"You're a grown man now, Hitch, but I still see you as the little guy knee-high to his dad when he brought you here when we first opened almost twenty years ago."

"This may surprise you, Bill, but I can remember Dad bringing me here before you bought this place, when it was Nick's BBQ—famous for the 'ham hamburgers' he made of smoked, ground ham."

"You have a good memory, Hitch."

"I'll remember you said that, Bill," he joked as he put cash on the counter and turned to leave.

Suddenly Bill snapped his fingers. "Ah! Don't go yet, Hitch. I almost forgot—one of the gals who works here wants to talk to you about something."

"Who?"

"The one you have your eye on every time you're here," Bill said as he slid a folded piece of paper across the counter.

Hitchcock felt his cheeks blush. "Oh? And which one would that be?" he asked with a sheepish smirk.

"Come on, you know who I mean," Bill said, laughing. "Allie, the little blonde all the guys come in just to feast their eyes on. She says its important and wants you to call her as soon as you can. She's off today. Said to give you her number if you came in."

"Is this business or personal?"

"Guess you'll have to find out." Bill winked as he headed to the back.

Hitchcock dropped a dime into the pay phone in the customer waiting area and dialed the number Bill gave him. He recognized Allie's voice when she answered.

"Hi Roger, thanks for calling." The musical lilt in her voice made him wonder if she sings.

"No problem, Allie, how can I help?"

He heard alarm in her voice when she said "I have information for you in case something happens to me. I won't say what it is on the phone. I have my son with me until my ex comes by about three hours from now for a visit. Can you meet me then?"

Right this second if you need me. "Absolutely. Tell me where and what time."

"My apartment is at Old Main Street and 100th Avenue, overlooking the lake."

"Two blocks from you is a bank."

"National Bank of Commerce?"

"That's the one. Meet you in the back parking lot at four o'clock. I'm in a gold El Camino."

Thoughts of Allie dominated his thoughts as he worked his Wednesday routine at the new Iron Works Gym on Northup Way. He went through his routine without stopping. Calisthenics, punching a heavy bag, skipping rope, a hundred pushups in four sets of twenty-five reps, light weights, and pull-ups. All the while he wondered what kind of trouble Allie could be in.

At Nick's BBQ on 104th Avenue, the main downtown drag, a block from where he would meet Allie, he wolfed down a green salad and a hunk of grilled beef brisket, medium rare. After his meal he parked in the back lot of the National Bank of Commerce and waited.

Other than casual chit-chat at the Corral, he didn't know Allie, but he couldn't help admiring her, a natural blonde with aquiline features and a perfect figure under a white waitress uniform. Add to that, her warm, pleasant personality refreshed everyone she met.

She pulled up in front of him ten minutes early in a tired gray Toyota sedan with bald tires.

His jaw fell open as Allie walked up to his passenger door. He had never before seen her in anything but a white waitress dress. *Women have cosmetic surgery to look half as good as Allie does without makeup*, he mentally remarked. Five-foot-one, petite, hourglass figure, full lips, exquisite features, she looked to be in her late teens or early twenties.

Poise and raw femininity oozed through her loose-fitting khakis as she sat in the passenger seat. Her oversized blue men's sweatshirt with paint stains, and unkempt neck-length genuinely golden hair indicated she had no social intentions, which disappointed him, to his surprise. *Where have I been? How could I have missed this?* he almost said out loud. She seemed like someone he had never seen before.

He tried to say hello, but no words came. A combination of sensuality and wholesomeness of the rarest order sat next to him, and all he could do was stare, dumbfounded. She smiled shyly at him.

"Thanks for meeting me, Roger," she said. "My ex can't stay with my son very long, so I'll be brief. There's this strange guy I believe is dangerous. I met him for coffee twice. Briefly both times. He keeps calling me, sometimes late at night and talks a lot of angry political stuff, trying to get me to see things from his point of view."

"Like?" He finally managed to ask.

"Poor working people like me have no chance because we're being exploited by the rich, who are protected by the police. He says the system is rigged against us and needs to be changed, and only violence will bring that change. I'm not into politics, so I don't say much in response, which I guess he must interpret as agreement, so he thinks I'm a candidate for his group."

"This group have a name?" he asked after clearing his throat.

"He never said. According to him they have guns and they intend to use them. Last week on my day off I met him for coffee at Ramona's, the café at the north end of town. He showed me his gun and told me his group is preparing for some kind of war. He had a military term for the group, but I can't remember it."

"He showed you a gun?"

She answered with a nervous nod.

"Inside the restaurant?"

"He made sure no one was looking."

He resisted the urge to reassure her by touching her hand. "You seem nervous. Are you all right?"

She hesitated. "This guy is so intense he scares me. I think he's trying to recruit me. I'm afraid of what will happen if I cut him off from calling."

"How and where did you meet him?"

"He kept coming into the Corral during the slow times, always alone and seeming down-and-out, like he needed someone to talk to. I have an infant son, so I don't date. I met him for coffee twice because I felt sorry for him. He seemed lonely and harmless, so I gave him my phone number. Big mistake."

"Then what happened?"

"He kept calling and wanting to meet. Every conversation is about politics. Radical, far-out stuff like robbing banks and state liquor stores to buy weapons to establish social justice. He says his name is Jim Randall, which I doubt." She handed Hitchcock a slip of paper. "Here's the phone number he gave me—I've never called it."

"Description?"

Allie hesitated, thinking. "About twenty-eight," she said, "brown hair to his shoulders, unshaved, pale skin. A down-and-out type."

"Thin, fat? Tall or short? Pimples or tattoos?"

"Umm…medium, five-nine or so, grimy hands like a mechanic."

"What does he drive?"

"An old gray foreign car of some type."

He pocketed the paper Allie gave him. "Just a name, with nothing else isn't much," he said, "but I'll get right on it. I'll let you know what I find out, either way."

Allie breathed a sigh of relief. "I knew I could count on you. Thank you, whatever the outcome is, Roger."

The electricity of her presence lingered as he watched her walk back to her beater car. He was mesmerized by her intense femininity and hourglass figure, which neither loose khaki pants nor oversize sweatshirt could hide.

On sudden impulse he tailed Allie to her apartment in case anyone followed her. No one did. He parked across the street and waited to what kind of fool would walk away from a fox like Allie.

Seconds after he saw Allie enter her second-floor apartment, a grungy, unshaven diminutive man stepped out of it. His appearance shocked Hitchcock. A pointed, rat-like face, greasy shoulder-length mouse-brown hair, scraggly mustache. Early thirties, maybe.

Though unkempt and shabbily dressed in a worn green ski parka and jeans, he had an air of snotty superiority in his bearing. Instead of a VW bus or some other typical hippie-rig, he drove away in a shiny new red Mercedes sedan.

The contrast between the Mercedes, the slovenly but snooty appearance of Allie's ex, and her grim financial status intrigued Hitchcock. He followed the Mercedes through three traffic signals until he could copy the plate number.

HIS SUDDEN ATTRACTION to Allie surprised him. He shook himself, then rationalized and dismissed his feelings as mere physical attraction to an unusually beautiful and vulnerable woman, nothing more.

Despite my God, country and family upbringing, the sudden death of dad, followed by life in a hot war zone where men around me were dying, made me too cynical to instantly fall for this love-at-first sight garbage. Whatever this is, I'll get over it, Besides, a ready-made family I don't need, he told himself.

Deer and elk hunting with his father, followed by war in Vietnam taught him about life's predators. Animal or human, predators hunt down and prey upon the weak, the helpless, the timid. The third, or sub category, are those who prey on the predators, the equivalent of sheepdogs.

He perceived a divine balance in the equation. On

the human level, citizens are sheep, life's givers and producers. They make for easy prey for the predators, the wolves, the takers and consumers in life, who range from common criminals to corrupt officials.

The third class, the sheepdogs—policemen and soldiers, are society's protectors. True sheepdogs don't just protect, they prey upon predators under the authority of a Divine Being. They are predators under the authority of Natural Law, to prey upon society's wolves.

Two years in a hot war zone and nine years of boxing taught him the world is hostile and the keys to survival and success in were discipline, vigilance, and a willingness to fight. In exercising these keys, Hitchcock had been faithful.

Boxing taught him the principle of muscle memory. Endless repetition enabled the body to react and perform when conscious effort collapsed. He applied this principle as a police officer. Every day before going to work, he practiced twenty-five slow, form-perfect draws from the holster, aiming at a piece of paper taped to the bedroom door at chest level with his empty service revolver.

It happened from years of boxing that speed and accuracy with his service weapon would come from constant repetition, so that in a crisis, his body would fight on its own, like cruise control.

Wednesday, 7:45 P.M.

CIGARETTE SMOKE PERMEATED the squad room as Hitchcock entered, officer's notebook in hand, and took a seat next to Otis. He noticed several new wanted posters on the back wall as the squad waited for Sergeant Breen, standing behind the podium, his nicotine-stained fingers flipping through the latest bulletins, to say something.

"First things first," Breen finally said without looking up at his troops. "It hasn't happened yet, but we can expect the newshounds to be all over last night's homicide and the pursuit which led to the suspect's arrest. If news people or anyone else contacts you about what happened last night, do *not* comment–period. Refer them to Captain Whittington, our new press information officer."

A round of scoffing whisked through the squad. "Dan Whittington is captain now? Who sobered him up enough to pass the exam?" Walker asked.

"Who said he had to be sober?" laughed Tom Sherman. The rest of the squad broke into snickering and scoffing.

"All right, pipe down," Sergeant Breen ordered. "We had our first murder last night and a high-risk pursuit to catch the killer. Such a dramatic event is bound to produce some change in our favor. Chief Carter is pleased with the outcome. He'll be fielding questions and complaints he's never had to deal with before, but he's up for it. From me, I say 'well done' to those of you who took huge risks to stop the suspect from killing more people."

Breen looked at his men before he added, "Also, I got word minutes ago that the second assault victim died this afternoon."

A hush fell over the squad. The officers glanced at each other, then returned their attention to Sergeant Breen, expecting more details.

"Hitchcock, Walker, Allard, and Sherman, I've put your names in for service commendations," Breen said. "Be sure to write your reports while the details are fresh in mind. It's Wednesday, so hopefully, it will be quiet tonight. I'll pick up your reports in the field. Diss-*missed!*"

CHAPTER THREE
Primitive Instincts

HITCHCOCK APPROACHED WALKER in the parking lot after shift briefing. "Meet me at the back of Charlie's right away. Radio silence."

"What's up?"

"Something tells me we should go there *now*."

"What about writing our reports as Breen told us?"

Hitchcock shook his head. "Charlie's. Trust me."

Walker stared wonderingly at Hitchcock for a second before he replied, "Sure thing, Roger."

Walker started toward his patrol car, then stopped. "Hold on, Roger—is this another one of your swami moments, like you had last night, before we even left the station?

Hitchcock nodded.

"Do I have time to call my life insurance agent to increase my coverage?"

Hitchcock laughed as he headed toward his cruiser.

"Meet you there, Ira."

A light rain fell as Hitchcock, with Walker following, sped toward Eastgate along Richards Road. He turned on his wipers. The new premonition was strong but undefined. He wondered what kind of trouble he'd find at Charlie's Place.

The parking lot was full when they arrived, which meant it was payday. He and Walker parked in the usual place–at the edge the pavement in the back lot, next to the Lakeside gravel pit and its heavy equipment.

They left their cruisers and met.

"Okay, Roger," Walker said, hitching up his gun belt, "what are we supposed to be here for?"

Hitchcock, unusually tense and alert, said nothing. Without another word they peered into pickups, station wagons and vans. Finding none occupied, they headed for the tavern.

A shaft of light, a blast of jukebox music, laughter and chattering voices inside pierced the night when the back door opened. A wiry, bearded young man in a red plaid shirt and dark knit cap stopped abruptly at the sight of two policemen approaching, then dashed back inside and slammed the door shut.

They sprinted to the back door as one man, holding their guns in their holsters with one hand, their batons in belt rings with the other. Hitchcock slipped inside first. He saw Wally Evans behind the bar, vigorously wiping the bar with a damp rag, making a show of pretending not to notice Hitchcock.

On full alert, Hitchcock stood a few feet inside, surveying the crowd of about forty, mostly men. The smells of wet canvas overalls, leather boots, automotive oil and grease, beer, cheap wine, cigarette smoke and fried food filled the air. Waylon Jennings sang *Brown Eyed Handsome Man* on the jukebox. Burly construction workers in canvas coats and ball caps relaxed around their tables, nursing their beers. Road workmen played pool. Mechanics in flannel shirts, grease under their fingernails, sleeves rolled up, played foosball.

A trim, thirtyish woman in a mini skirt bent over the jukebox, elbows on the glass cover, reading the menu of songs. Two couples in their forties stood by the front door, beers in hand, chatting. An especially attractive blonde woman in her forties sat between two men in their early fifties, smiling and talking with them equally, pleased by the hunger for her in their eyes.

Hitchcock's eyes scanned every corner. No bearded man in the red plaid shirt.

Debbie, the blonde barmaid, wore a worried expression as she waited on tables. He took it as another sign of trouble when she cast a fearful glance at him without her usual smile.

He felt his pulse increase. Something was wrong. The man who fled from him and Walker had disappeared. The front door was shut. There hadn't been enough time for the man to go out the front door, and besides, two couples stood in front of it, talking and drinking.

Hitchcock pressed his elbow against the grip of his revolver as he moved further into the tavern and scanned the darkest corners a second time. No bearded man in a red plaid shirt anywhere. Walker blocked the rear door, thumbs hooked into his gun belt, eyes on Hitchcock's back and what he could see of the customers, including the front door.

Wally kept wiping the same spot on the bar, his eyes avoiding Hitchcock when he approached.

"What can I do for you, *officer*?"

"How are things tonight, *bartender*?" Hitchcock replied, acknowledging Wally's coded warning.

"Oh, just another quiet Wednesday, *officer*," Wally said, his voice cracking as his eyes motioned to the women's restroom located next to the back door. "You *understand* how nights like these are, *officer*..." Wally's voice trailed off as his eyes motioned to the left a second time, still rubbing the counter with his towel.

"Very well, then. Have a good evening, *bartender*," Hitchcock said as he turned toward the women's restroom, drawing his gun. With a "cover me" nod to Walker, he tried the door. Someone was blocking it from the inside.

He knocked. No response. He pushed the door again. It wasn't locked–someone on the other side was holding it shut.

"Police! I know you're in there! Come out now."

No answer.

Keeping his finger out of the trigger guard of his revolver, Hitchcock put his left shoulder against the door and leaned against it until it gave. Into the closet-sized restroom he went, gun first. The force knocked the man inside against the opposite wall.

"Don't shoot, officer. I'm clean," the man hissed.

Instead of a beard and red jacket, this man was clean-shaven, blue denim shirt and jeans. His face was angular and pointy, his build small and wiry, but hard like spring steel; a quick, deadly ferret in human form.

"Hands up, no funny business," Hitchcock commanded.

Reptilian eyes set in a human skull assessed Hitchcock. The man grinned as he raised his open hands in one smooth motion. The space inside was too tight to frisk him for weapons without risking a struggle for his gun, so Hitchcock grabbed the front of his shirt with his left hand and pulled him close as he pressed the barrel of his revolver under his chin. The suspect's eyes widened with alarm when Hitchcock stared into him and cocked the hammer. *Click.*

"Now—we're going out of here together, like this, in small steps. Keep your hands up, without fail." Hitchcock said in a low voice. He walked slowly backward, his finger on the trigger, pulling the suspect step-by-step out of the restroom, each man staring intently into the other.

He saw in the suspect's eyes a cornered predator, a cold lethality he hadn't seen since Vietnam. His gut instinct told him he held the power of life or death over a killer. Having been in combat before, Hitchcock made up his mind to pull the trigger if he had to in order to keep the upper hand.

Someone unplugged the jukebox. A hush fell over the tavern. The crowd got to its feet as Hitchcock and his prisoner inched their way into the open and a deafening quiet.

Hitchcock holstered his gun as Walker cuffed the suspect's hands behind him. Walker patted him down for weapons, finding a thin, flat, long-blade knife, the prison-made kind, the hilt wrapped with black electrician's tape, scotch-taped upside down to his bare chest under his shirt. His pockets held nothing except a few crumpled one-dollar bills and some change. No wallet, no ID.

"Who are you and what's going on here?" Walker demanded.

The human ferret said nothing. Hitchcock returned to the restroom. In the wastebasket, hidden under a pile of paper towels, he found a red plaid flannel shirt, a black knit cap, a fake beard, and a General Motors car key. On the bottom of the trashcan, under a pile of used paper towels he found a loaded 9mm Browning Hi-Power pistol. Hitchcock returned to the suspect, keeping the pistol out of view. He held the beard, cap, and shirt up to the suspect's face.

"Start talking."

The suspect bowed his head in refusal. His coolness in conjunction with the gun and the disguise led Hitchcock to conclude that by changing their usual routine, he and Walker had averted a mass armed robbery.

Walker took the prisoner to his patrol car while Hitchcock got the names and phone numbers of the customers.

Wally was white-faced and shaking. "*This* is the guy who was here last night. The one I told you about, Roger! Same guy!"

"What happened tonight?"

Wally placed both palms of his meaty hands on the bar. He stared at Hitchcock for several seconds. Hitchcock, seeing fear in Wally's eyes, waited.

"He walked in about an hour ago, a few minutes before eight actually," Wally said after clearing his throat. "Sat in the corner, watching. Had one beer, never said a word. Just before you arrived, he went to the front door. I thought he was going to leave but he didn't. He went out the back door instead, which I thought was odd. A split-second later he ran back in and ducked into the women's restroom. Even before he came in, I had the same bad feeling I had last night. I mean, *really* bad, and I didn't know he was the same guy as last night because of–" Wally gestured to the wig, fake beard and change of clothing.

Hitchcock used the phone behind the bar to call Sergeant Breen while Wally sent the rest of his customers away.

"YOU GOT NOTHING to hold me for," the suspect argued from the back of Walker's cruiser. "I've committed no crime. Better let me go or you'll be hearing from my attorney."

"Give it a rest, pal," Walker responded. "Relax. You're in good hands now–ours."

With renewed urgency in his voice the suspect demanded "What's the charge? Huh? You can't hold me without a charge. So tell me—what's the charge?"

"Don't worry, we'll cook something up."

"This isn't funny, officer."

Walker snapped his fingers. "I got it! You're under arrest for First Degree B.A.I.B."

"What?"

"Being An Idiot In Bellevue."

The suspect snorted and shook his head as he gazed out the window.

The back door of Walker's cruiser opened suddenly. Hitchcock jerked the suspect out of the cruiser by his shirt. "Here's how it is: I'm arresting you for unlawful carrying of a concealed weapon. Now, who are you and how did you get here?"

Twisting his wrists within the handcuffs behind him, the prisoner shook his head. "The gun wasn't on me, officer," he snickered. "You got nothing, and I don't have to tell you who I am," he said, confidence in his voice.

"Well, well! *Who* said anything about a gun? *You* did! By your own words, the gun is yours. Thank you very much," Hitchcock said in a tone of mock cheer.

The suspect grimaced and glanced at the ground, visibly upset at his mistake, shifting his feet and his wrists within the handcuffs.

Hitchcock tried taunting him into talking more. "I wasn't referring to the gun anyway—it's the knife."

"Not illegal in Washington!!"

"In *my* district, it is. I'm betting we'll find your prints on the gun and the front door latch, where you intended to hold everybody hostage and rob each one at gunpoint. You're probably wanted somewhere too, from the look of you."

"No more talk. I want an attorney."

Walker smiled as he put his hand on the suspect's shoulder. "Let's trade. You tell us your name at least, and I'll unarrest you for being an idiot. What do you say?"

Hitchcock finished taking written statements from Wally and Debbie. By then the parking lot was empty except for one car. The key he found with the gun and the disguise fit the remaining car, a well-maintained, white, late '60s Pontiac sedan registered to a Harper Wilcox with a Yakima address, over a hundred miles across the state.

Walker headed for the station with the suspect.

To keep reporters and police wannabes from listening in, Hitchcock used the phone in Wally's office to call in the license number of the Pontiac to Records. In seconds Patty advised that the Pontiac wasn't stolen, that the registered owner, Harper Wilcox, was fifty-two–too old to be the guy in the back of Walker's cruiser.

"Okay. Walker's bringing the suspect to the station," he replied. "He has no ID on him and won't identify himself. Call the registered owner. Ask him who is supposed to have his car. I'll be at the station in a few."

The impound truck would arrive soon. Hitchcock went through the contents of the Pontiac. He found a half-empty fifty-round box of 9mm ammunition and another pistol magazine loaded with thirteen rounds in the glove box. He sorted through cash receipts and matchbooks from various bars, restaurants, and motels in a cigar box he found under the front seat.

Two receipts from The Great Wall caught his eye. One from last night–the time stamped only an hour before he and Walker stopped by and talked to Juju. The other receipt brought a shock—it had been time-stamped at The Great Wall *just over an hour ago.*

A small crowd from the tavern gathered outside, huddled in the misty rain, keeping a respectful distance, watching and murmuring.

Sergeant Breen arrived. He stared out his windshield, hands on his steering wheel, his face stoic as he listened to Hitchcock's summary of events.

"There's nothing we can arrest Juju for," Breen said when Hitchcock finished.

"Juju's in this up to her eyeballs, Sarge, she lied to me and Walker last night when she told us no one matching the suspect's description had ever been in her place, yet one of his receipts place him at Juju's while we were at shift briefing."

"It's not a crime to lie to us, like it is to the feds" Breen said. "All we have on the mystery man are misdemeanors. It's a major red flag for a woman of Juju's financial status and position in the community to be connected to an illegally armed guy from out-of-town, but not a crime."

"The only things Wally and Juju have in common are their businesses are on the same road and serve drinks," Hitchcock said. "Charlie's Place caters to rednecks—the evening customers of The Great Wall are well-to-do Orientals from Seattle. They only drink there, never eat, which says they know something about the food. The restaurant does little business."

"Anything else?" Breen asked after a thoughtful pause.

"Juju has an eye for men."

"She's legendary for that," Sergeant Breen said, stoic as always. "She's a man-eater."

"That's my point. Juju always greets male customers, more so if they're alone," Hitchcock pursued. "Our mystery man was at her place when we know she was there last night. She lied to us about not seeing him."

Breen nodded, still looking out his windshield. "Again, there's still nothing to arrest Juju for," he said. "Keep digging. The prisoner's intent was either robbery or a hit job on somebody he expected to be there. Maybe what we learn about the prisoner or from him will enable us to arrest Juju later. Do everything you can to identify him."

At that, Sergeant Breen left.

As Hitchcock sealed the doors and windows of the Pontiac with evidence tape, he spotted an electronic device mounted way up under the dash on the transmission hump. He cursed when he turned it on and heard calls being dispatched on Frequency One.

A truck from Ibsen Towing arrived. "Keep it in secure storage on police hold. The dicks'll get a search warrant tomorrow," he told the driver.

"THE SUSPECT REMAINS silent," Walker told Hitchcock when he entered the booking room., "won't say who he is." Hitchcock nodded as he headed to the nearest phone and called Records.

"I called the registered owner of the vehicle, Harper Wilcox, of Yakima," clerk Patty Hooper reported. "He told me he loaned the car to his nephew, Colin, when he was paroled from the state pen at Walla Walla six months ago."

"Anything else?"

"Colin Wilcox, age thirty-seven, is confirmed as wanted by the Department of Corrections for parole violation."

"What was he in for?"

"He served three years of a ten-year sentence for murder in Yakima County, reduced to manslaughter," Patty said. "His rap sheet includes multiple arrests for burglary and armed robbery in Yakima, Chelan and Spokane counties, most of which were plea-bargained down or away. He has quite a history of trips to Chicago in his file."

That caught Hitchcock's attention. "Call the owner of the Pontiac again. Ask him if he would talk to Colin for a minute. If he agrees, transfer the call to me in the booking room."

Five minutes later the booking room phone rang. Hitchcock answered, listened, then said, "Just a second." He handed the phone to the suspect. "It's for you."

The surprised suspect took the phone. "Hello?"

After a few seconds of silence, the suspect said, "All

right, I will." He handed the phone back to Hitchcock.

"Officer Hitchcock here."

"I'm Harper Wilcox, officer, the owner of the Pontiac you're calling about. The man I just spoke to is my nephew, Colin. I told him to tell you his name and other information. If he doesn't, call me back."

Hitchcock turned to the suspect after the call ended. "No point in keeping up the mystery anymore, is there?"

Wilcox gave only identifying information. Another officer took him to the county jail.

THE RESTAURANTS AND bars were closing when Hitchcock returned to Eastgate, tired and grateful that the radio was quiet. He parked under the bright lights of the closed Sunset Bowl to write his report. Walker pulled up as he finished.

"So, what do you think, Roger: Why would a professional hit man with no history of being in Western Washington, violate his parole by coming here and hang around Eastgate for who-knows-how-long?"

Hitchcock stared through the windshield and shook his head. "The disguises and the gun tell me Wilcox went there to do a hit, maybe on Wally, the owner. He's from Chicago, you know."

"Whoa. You think the Chicago mob put out a contract on Wally? You've been reading too many detective novels."

"Maybe Wilcox went there to shoot somebody he expected to come through the door," Hitchcock speculated. "It would account for the disguises and sitting by the door both times."

"Wrong. He locked the front door so no one could come in, Roger."

Hitchcock paused. "That leaves robbery as the motive. *Somebody* is paying his expenses. He had less than ten bucks in his pocket, so what has he been living on?"

"Other than Juju, no clue. To be fair, all he did was eat at Juju's place twice."

"Why did Wilcox go straight to Charlie's Place from Juju's two nights in a row, and where did he get the gun?"

"Maybe he used the gun to shoot the deer you saw last night in Juju's kitchen," Walker said with a smirk. "Times *are* tight, you know!"

"I got it—he stole his uncle's piggy bank, came here to start over, and just happens to love Chinese food."

"Sounds like a ploy a defense attorney would try."

"Yeah? Play the defense," Hitchcock challenged.

"Ahem. Ladies and gentlemen of the jury, the prosecutor would have you believe the defendant went to The Great Wall twice out of his preference for Chinese food, which can't be had in Yakima," Walker sportively stated.

"The truth is, ladies and gentlemen," countered

Hitchcock as the prosecutor, "that the State Health Department's records will back me up with documents of customer complaints and suspensions of license, anybody who loves Chinese food would eat at The Great Wall *only once!*"

Walker beat his head on the steering wheel, chuckling. "Touché! Court adjourned. You destroyed the defense in a single sentence. Bravo."

"Still," Hitchcock asked, "why would Wilcox come all the way from Yakima and go to Charlie's Place twice, wearing disguise, armed with a gun?"

CHAPTER FOUR
Codes of Honor

THREE SOFT KNOCKS on Hitchcock's apartment door the next afternoon meant a woman was outside. He met a frizzy-haired hippie chick in her early twenties, wearing a nervous smile when he opened the door.

"Hey, Roger-man, I'm Willow, your upstairs neighbor. I think you're kinda cool and macho, and uh, well, I wanna give you Ollie, my pet rock, so your rock, Ollie, and my rock, Fawn, can date, you dig?"

He had to smile at her. Tall, scrawny and pale, her bulging blue eyes and kinky light brown hair sticking straight out gave her a weird, electrifying look. But for all that, he had to admit, Willow was a looker.

She held out a flat stone painted lime green with a smiling face in white with pink lips. Dumbfounded, he could only reply, "Huh?"

"Yeah, see, my rock is a girl, Fawn Rainforest, and this is Ollie, a rock-guy, and Ollie is going to miss his rock-woman after I give him to you. So, maybe we could put them together for a date at my place upstairs, say Saturday night?"

Such a creative approach for a woman to ask a strange man for a date impressed him. "Gee thanks, Willow," he replied kindly, his face smiling, "but I'll have to take a raincheck. I'm working the night shift now and Saturday is my Monday. Thanks, though, for giving me Ollie–this is very thoughtful of you. I'll take care of him. Maybe next month we can get together."

Willow stuck her lower lip out and fluttered her eyelids. "Bummer. You might want to come. This Saturday will be special."

"Oh? How so?"

"My friends are bringing some mice or rats from the pet store. We take bets on the time it takes my boa to eat the rodents we drop in the cage one at a time while we drink rose wine take bets on how much time my boa takes to eat them."

"Are you putting me on?" he asked, astounded.

"Trust me, it's not a drag, not at all," Willow said, "but sadly, the apartment manager found out about my snake and told me to get rid of it by Monday or move out, so this weekend is your last chance to see the show."

"Aha!" Hitchcock said, still shocked. "Well, thanks anyway, Willow, for the pet rock and the invite."

Remembering snakes slithering among him and his fellow soldiers as they slept on the ground when they were on missions in Vietnam, Hitchcock began searching for a house or a cabin to rent–no more apartment living.

ONLY ON THURSDAYS did the Pancake Corral open for dinner, serving a limited menu of hamburgers and Louise's homemade New England-style chili and cornbread. Hitchcock, who loved simple grub, stopped by to check on Allie, whose schedule he made a point of knowing, as well as to partake in the home-style cuisine.

Who should he see there but the town veterinarian, Doc Henderson, and his wife, Ethel. Seeing Doc brought back the time when his father took him to Doc's clinic to pick out his first dog. He chose a handsome golden Collie like in the movies and named him Champ.

He accepted Doc's invitation to sit with them. Allie took over as their waitress as they caught up on family news. As he knew they would, Doc and Ethel reminisced about his father. When he mentioned his housing dilemma, Doc and Ethel offered their cabana.

"Follow us home to see it. We're two minutes from the police station. You'll be set. Only one bedroom, but it has a fireplace, kitchen, bath, all the privacy you need. A steal for fifty bucks a month," Doc said, warmth in his eyes.

He followed Doc and Ethel's metallic root beer brown Lincoln Continental down a quarter mile of tree-lined, single-lane gravel road to the Henderson's late 1940s vintage home. The seclusion in the midst of fifteen impenetrable wooded acres reminded him of his boyhood home in a similar setting.

The cabana was adjacent to the carport and connected to the house by a covered patio. The next day, a delighted Hitchcock prepaid the next two month's apartment rent and gave his key to Walker, who needed a place of his own.

After moving his few furnishings in, he built a crackling fire in the fireplace, brewed a pot of strong coffee and put his feet up as he got into re-reading Jack London's *Call of the Wild*. At last, he had digs as nonconforming as himself. All he needed now was the right dog.

† † †

LIFE WAS CHANGING fast for Colin Wilcox. The hitman sat in his cell in the King County Jail, reviewing his life. He prided himself as a *professional* criminal. As such, he adhered to a code that understood and accepted that occasional arrest and confinement were occupational hazards that came with the territory.

He thought of himself as a soldier of fortune, a gun for hire. As such, remorse of any kind was beneath him as a true mercenary. To his credit, Wilcox never blamed his behavior on his childhood, teachers or parents. He regarded those who did as weak snivelers without honor.

How such a hardened criminal could come from a

warm and stable home baffled everyone who knew the family. Wilcox grew up in a close-knit clan of farmers in the Yakima Valley. Rock-steady, church-going parents, uncles, aunts and cousins plus four siblings, of whose deep grief he was the main cause.

Somehow, a perverted sense of honor influenced Wilcox's conduct from his teen years. He strove to be the best in whatever crime category was his specialty at the time. As he progressed from shoplifting to daytime home burglary to commercial burglary, he researched the richest and easiest targets, studied police methods of evidence gathering, crime prevention, security patrols and alarms. He even worked as an apprentice locksmith for a season to learn the art of safecracking.

He applied the same standards of discipline when he moved up to armed robbery and finally murder-for-hire because the money was better. He learned knife fighting and bare hand killing techniques while in prison. He owned an assortment of weapons. When not in jail or prison, he practiced police-style combat shooting with his treasured blued Colt Detective Special, snub-nose .38 revolver and his Colt Army 1911 .45 Automatic.

Wilcox played his cards close to his vest. He never confided in anyone, never bragged about himself or his exploits. His reputation for daring deeds preceded him in the underworld, which led to higher fees. He held an adversarial respect for the police based on experience and his view of himself as a professional criminal. He never mocked or taunted policemen—true professionals never stoop to that, only punks. But he had to admit, the times were changing.

It dismayed Wilcox to see his brand of criminal, who lived by a certain code of conduct, fading from the scene. Even in the underworld, a new order was sweeping aside the old, replacing it with a new breed of criminal: politically oriented and driven, drug-addicted, Marxist and revolutionary in viewpoint, hating the Establishment, bent on anarchy.

The way his arrest went down baffled Wilcox. What happened that the cops arrived at Charlie's Place an hour earlier than usual? He knew their patrol patterns well after weeks of surveillance. They *had* to have been tipped off.

To reduce the risk of being betrayed, he had withheld the details of his plans, especially the date and time of his strike from even his client. When he gave it more thought, there was too much the police *didn't* do, for him to believe he had been sold out. If the police had advance information that he would be there and what for, there would have been a team of plain clothes cops inside, waiting. But instead, only the same two beat cops showed up.

Having thought the matter through, Wilcox chalked his arrest up to bad luck—nothing more. His only *good* luck was being still alive because he correctly read the cop who arrested him.

In his own twisted way, Wilcox felt honored that the arresting officer took him seriously, as a peer. The young lawman didn't overreact. That he had killed before was obvious, most likely while in the military. Wilcox judged correctly that the patrolman wouldn't hesitate to kill him—nor would it bother him if he did. Wilcox believed the lawman drew his gun out of recognition and respect, as one serious life-taker to another, a notion that satisfied Wilcox's ego.

The state's no-bail holds for parole violation and felon in possession of a firearm that were sure to come didn't worry Wilcox. He wouldn't be in jail long. To the contrary, he relaxed because of the phone call he made from the county jail. It wasn't to his uncle in Yakima.

SCHEDULE PERMITTING, HITCHCOCK took his mother to lunch every Friday at the elegant Rhododendron Room in the Frederick & Nelson department store in Bellevue Square. The décor had the feel of a 1930s classic film: deep, maroon floral-pattern carpet, plush, high-back maroon leather booths, crystal chandeliers, white tablecloths, genuine sterling silver flatware, miniature palm trees in gleaming pottery, strategically placed.

The waiters and waitresses wore starched white dress shirts with barrel cuffs and black slacks or skirts, a

style and sense of class that was vanishing fast in the
'70s. Hitchcock imagined a saxophone playing every
time he entered, and seeing movie actor Humphrey
Bogart sitting in a booth, wearing his trademark trench
coat and fedora hat.

As he expected, Myrna started in as soon as the
waitress seated them. Being the dutiful son, he allowed
her to chide him, knowing his father would be pleased.

"Roger, your dad would have wanted you to be in
medical school by now," she began. "Like him, you'd be
so well-suited for medicine. Remember how in high
school you always got A's in biology and chemistry?
Your father felt sure you would follow in his footsteps
one day. He wouldn't have wanted you in the Army, let
alone on the police force, of all things," Myrna said,
shaking her head.

"But Mom, I *am* following Dad's lead. He left
medical school during the war to join the Army,
remember? And where did he wind up? On the beach at
Normandy on D-Day, as a medic. He got wounded
there. So, I left medical school to join the Army, where I
was a medic, like him."

"Oh yes, but those were different times," Myrna
replied. "We were dating then. I thought I would die
when Ted left medical school to go fight in a war. He got
wounded. He could have been killed!" Myrna said with
a dismissive wave of her hand.

He unfolded the white linen napkin and smoothed

it on his lap. He toyed with the sterling silverware as he waited for his mother's tirade to end.

"And, Roger, you should be thinking about starting a family, while you're still young. I do hope you're past the fling you had with the...the blonde cow *woman-thing* who sent you a Dear John letter while you were a soldier, fighting for the country. I've got just the girl for you, a good girl from a very well-to-do family. They go to our church."

A smile came over Hitchcock's face as he wondered how his mother's choice for him would stack up against Allie, the humble little waitress who happened to be a 15 on a scale of 10 in every department.

He shook his head. "Someone on the Department is getting married every month, Mom. Mostly they're marrying girls they met on the job. They're buying homes and having babies. Not me. Not anymore."

When Myrna became silent, he knew what her next subject would be. "As you know, your sisters and I don't think this police business is for you. You have a higher calling."

"You've told me this before, Mom," was his gentle return.

"Besides the poor pay, the work is dangerous," Myrna went on, ignoring her son's remark. "Why, Irene, my hairdresser, says policemen aren't popular anymore, which of course is really too bad. She says they're actually being *attacked* in some places! Just what is this world coming to, anyway?" She asked, shaking her head.

The waitress brought their orders. He didn't close his eyes when his mother offered a prayer over the meal.

"Society's under deliberate attack from within like never before, Mom. The only thing preventing a collapse into anarchy is the police presence," he said.

Myrna shook her forefinger in his face. "So, Roger, you see, the best thing is for you to quit risking your life for people who don't like you and don't deserve the risks you take for them, and go back to college, and I'll introduce you to the Chatterton girl."

He gave no reply.

"Oh, I almost forgot—when you meet her, don't mention anything about being a boxer, but baseball is okay. Her family is opposed to violence, including sports. Don't worry, they're not Quakers. But don't talk about your fighting in Vietnam. Or arresting people, either."

"Well, Mom, what's left for me to talk about with such fine, important folks? The hottest bowling matches coming up? No, wait. I'm sure bowling is too blue-collar for them. How about the latest knitting tournament? Or the national spelling bee competition?"

"Stop with the teasing!" Myrna said, waving her hand. "You'll thank me when you meet the Chatterton girl." She placed her hand over her heart and bowed her head in melodramatic reverence.

Inwardly, he shook his head, thinking *Mom, Mom, oh Mom*, he commented mentally. Rather than argue, he changed the subject to divert her endless efforts to reattach her apron strings.

He took his mother home after lunch and did chores around her place before leaving. On his way to the Iron Works Gym, he stopped at a pay phone to call Allie to see if she was all right. She'd had no more calls from the mysterious Jim Reynolds. He spent the evening on a date with Eve from the prosecutor's office and arrived home late.

He slept in as late as possible as he always did on Saturdays. He ate, showered and re-read a short story by one of his favorite authors, O. Henry, before returning to work, happy to be a free man.

SATURDAY NIGHTS DURING the holidays often stretched the nine-man squad beyond its capacity to answer non-emergency calls. The ringing of cash registers in the bars and no-tell motels went on without letup.

Taxis ferried drugs, alcohol and call girls to private parties, officers broke up parking lot fights, raided underage drinking parties in homes, abandoned houses and the woods when they spiraled out of control. Traffic units responded to accident scenes and arrested drunk drivers and went off duty at 10:00 p.m.

Pot, cocaine and heroin were openly consumed in public. In some bars, live rock and country music bands pounded and pulsed, and fist fights over women abounded.

This particular Saturday felt to Hitchcock like musical chairs with handcuffs all night without letup. When the holding cells were full, officer safety had to be risked further by taking two officers off the streets to transport prisoners to the county jail in Seattle. But the mayhem pleased the third shift officers because the pressure proved the city's tangible need for protection and refuted the City Manager's scornful comments.

JUST AFTER 2:00 in the morning, when the streets began to clear, Hitchcock got a completed suicide call:

He arrived at the split-level home in less than five minutes. The front door was ajar. The familiar sounds of unspeakable grieving within beckoned him to enter.

"Hello inside the house! Police officer! I'm coming in!" He entered, the stairs creaking with each step. A grief-stricken woman in her forties lay in a fetal position on the kitchen floor, groaning and sobbing uncontrollably, tears streaming over her pain-contorted face. Her husband knelt over her, doing his best to console her, though his own grief limited what he could do.

Deeply moved, Hitchcock knelt next to the man, and, putting his hand on his shoulder, he spoke gently. "I am here for you, sir. How can I help?"

"It's—it's—our son," he said, halting, choking on and through tears. "We came home tonight and found him dead. He's downstairs…in his room…" The broken father's voice trailed off.

He descended two short staircases to the basement. What he saw overwhelmed him. A young man in his twenties hung by his neck from a rope tied to the ceiling joist, his feet dangling about twenty inches above the floor. He wore a military haircut, pressed Marine Corps dress greens, National Defense and Vietnam Campaign ribbons attached to the left breast of his uniform, spit-shined shoes gleaming in the dim light.

In addition to the dress uniform, the scene showed other signs of planning. The victim used the pointed compass handsaw on the floor to cut holes in the ceiling on either side of the ceiling joist, around which he looped one end of a length of half-inch manila rope. He fashioned a loop with a slipknot, the hangman's noose, stood on a chair, put the rope around his neck and kicked the chair away.

Purplish postmortem lividity darkened his neck, face and hands. His unseeing eyes were half-open slits, and his tongue protruded from his contorted face, purplish black. Hitchcock felt his hands. Cold to the touch.

Hitchcock crossed the room to the thermostat that read sixty-eight degrees. He felt fading warmth when he placed his hand under the Marine's armpit, indicating death occurred between two and four hours ago.

A handwritten note, pinned to the lapel of his uniform jacket, read:

> *Mom and Dad,*
> *Please forgive me for this and try*
> *to understand. I have chosen to go be*
> *with my unit, where I belong.*
> *I love you both, Kyle.*

Fighting a surge of raw emotion, Hitchcock returned to the parents, where the father told him: "Our son, our only child, joined the Marines against our wishes. He dreamed of being a Marine all through his boyhood. When his unit shipped out to Vietnam a year ago, my wife was beside herself. We pulled some string through her congressman uncle to bring him home, an early release, against *his* wishes."

The father broke into sobbing. Rubbing his palms on his knees and wiping his eyes with his sleeves, he patted his wife on the back as she continued to lie on the floor. He managed to pull himself together enough to say, "The day after Kyle left Vietnam, his entire unit was wiped out in an ambush. He never forgave us for bringing him home early. Never got over his guilt. Back here at home, it broke him to be called a baby-killer. Even his high school friends said horrible things to him. Counseling never helped. Now we are…"

The impact of the dead Marine, his parents, and the

treatment he got from his peers made Hitchcock's blood run hot. Under his uniform his flesh quivered as troubling thoughts swept through him.

The sneering indifference of the society he came back to was bad enough. In Phu Loi, a team of journalists and photographers on assignment from Life magazine feigned friendliness to the troops for information. Their twisted coverage made zero mention of the aid, protection and help American soldiers often did for suffering Vietnamese civilians. Such men not only scorned the sacrifices of better men than themselves, they made heroes of deserters, draft dodgers, potheads and flag desecrators.

He choked back his bitterness as he briefed Sergeant Breen and the coroner's investigator when they arrived. He nodded his approval when he heard Breen instruct Dispatch to call the police chaplain in to help the parents.

Someone had to honor this young Marine, even if it was posthumously. Hitchcock got his eight-point billed hat from his car and returned to the body, where he stood at attention, holding a salute as the coroner's investigator and Sergeant Breen took the body down.

After helping cover and remove the body from the house, he remained with the parents until the police chaplain arrived.

Hitchcock's rawest emotions surfaced as he cleared the call. He felt depleted. The past was calling him, and he needed to go home to face the scenes alone. Like the dead Marine, he had left Vietnam, but Vietnam would never leave him. He wanted solitude. He struggled to advise Radio he was back in service.

Luckily, the calls he received for the rest of his shift were few and minor.

The squad would be meeting at Jason Allard's for post-shift drinking, a frequent event which often lasted for hours. Even Walker, whose divorce was days from becoming final, would be going. Needing solitude, he declined.

When he reached the seclusion of his cabana, he locked the sliding glass door and drew the blinds, for he wanted darkness. He removed his gun belt and uniform, unplugged the phone, got a glass tumbler and his bottle of Old No. 7. He turned out the lights and sat in his underwear on the couch, drinking, grieving for the dead young Marine, a patriot cheated out of fulfilling his code of honor, and for his parents, who did the cheating, but out of love for their only son.

There were no winners—only losers. A valiant young man pulled against his will from a war he willingly volunteered for, and prepared for, only to face a different war at home. A crueler war he wasn't prepared for, in which he died repeatedly, defenseless at the hands and words of former friends who were now enemies. With his fellow Marines, who were already dead, he would not be alone—he would be with them again, for they understood—it was the warrior code. No wonder then, that he chose to rejoin them. His well-meaning parents, God bless them, were as good as dead, never to recover.

As he refilled his glass, Hitchcock's musings took him back, as he knew they would, to scenes he would relive forever. He knew where the dead Marine's thoughts had driven him.

He had to be alone, in the dark, when the faces of Phu Loi and scenes of his second tour returned. Buddies he had been unable to save appeared again. He heard again the screams of wounded and dying soldiers, some he knew by name, others not. The faces of the pitiful villagers they treated—against orders, out of compassion–and the enemies he slew, he saw again.

He slugged down another glass and resumed his first tour. Maybe they're the lucky ones. *They won't suffer returning home to be spit on and called names instead of being honored,* he thought bitterly.

He poured another three fingers of whiskey and drank, reliving the faces and events of his second tour, never to be forgotten, never to be discussed. Not with anyone.

He continued drinking, reliving scenes of death and dying until his head spun and sleep overtook him where he sat.

CHAPTER FIVE
A Case of Womanly Intuition

ANOTHER WOMAN'S KNOCKING brought him out of another skirmish in the jungle. He awoke and looked around. He was still on his couch. His throat felt dry, his sweat-drenched T-shirt stuck to his skin like flypaper. The knocking continued. A light rapping–that of a woman, no doubt.

He flung the blinds open and did a double-take at the well-assembled woman on his patio, dressed in a figure-hugging gray sweater dress, high-heels, pearl necklace. Rhonda. He had only seen her before in hospital scrubs and stethoscope or jeans and western-style flannel shirts with pearl snap buttons.

He opened the sliding glass door.

"Hi, babe," she said, smiling like a wife as she stepped inside. "I just got out of church and came by to take you to a late breakfast."

"I need to shower first," he said, squinting.

"Hmmm. Had a one-man party after work, did you?" she said, eyeing the near-empty bottle, the whiskey glass and the full ashtray. "Hit the shower while I tidy up a bit." She caressed his shoulder and tiptoed up to kiss him, then stepped back. "You do need a shower, my love," she said, giving him a gentle push.

He showered and dressed quickly, skipping the shave to save time. Rhonda's surprise visit pleased him. Her country-girl charm and frontier warmth brightened everyone she met. He appreciated her uniqueness, an outdoor cowgirl type, a down-home, freckle-faced MD packed into a pleasing figure.

"Where're we off to?"

"A place you haven't been to before," she said, putting her new Suburban in gear.

He looked her over. "I like how you look today, dressed as you are."

She smiled again, taking her eyes off the road to glance at him. "Thanks. I'm wearing it for church, and you—not necessarily in that order."

After last night's shift, Rhonda's comments were to him like cool water in a parched land. The flowing quality of her voice flooded over him, cooling and refreshing. She turned in to a parking lot and stopped in front of a one-story brick house converted into a restaurant. He came out of his reverie and looked around.

"We're in Redmond, Roger," she said. "My friends

own this place. They closed an hour ago but they're expecting us."

The smells of oregano, rosemary, and garlic greeted his nostrils as he stepped into a warmly lit, Mediterranean setting. A plump, fortyish, pleasant-looking Italian woman in a gingham dress greeted Rhonda with a hug.

"Thank you for staying open jut for us, Francesca," Rhonda said as she gestured to Hitchcock. "This is Roger, the man I've been telling you about."

Francesca turned to Hitchcock with a beaming smile and a hearty handshake, she said, "So glad-a to-a meet-chu! My dear Rhonda, here, she talk-a 'bout-chu a lotta!"

His eyes swept the warm, old world elegance around him. "Beautiful restaurant. I just got here and I feel right at home."

"Yess-a, we closed-a da place an hour ago, but we open now only for Rhonda, and-a you!" Francesca said with loving eyes. "Please, you two sit here," she said, gesturing to a booth upholstered in wine red leather and a starched white linen tablecloth.

First came Ribollita, a hearty vegetable peasant soup, then sumptuous samplings of lasagna, risotto, thin slices of Fiorintina steak, Bottarga-smoked fish eggs that were like caviar, and carbonara were set before them in courses. It put the canned man-chow he lived on to shame.

He gazed at her as she ate. She was thirty, seven years

older than himself, but with her smooth skin and youthful features she could pass for twenty-one. He recalled how they laughed when a waiter asked for her ID when she ordered a glass of wine on their first date. Like him, she had never been married, but her reasons were medical school and internship—his were different.

Thoughts of last night's dead Marine call crept into his thoughts, but Rhonda's talk brought him back. "You never talk about Vietnam. As a medic there you must have seen a lot. Is it all right for me to ask about it?"

His gaze fell to his plate. He toyed with his fork and shrugged. "Not much to tell. I did two tours. The first time in a sort of a mini-MASH unit in a place called Phu Loi, in the jungle—sort of an ER closer to the battlefields. We treated the wounded before getting them to the hospital at Long Binh. We operated under crude conditions. South Vietnamese medical personnel were there for their soldiers."

"And the second time?"

He hesitated. "I wasn't at Phu Loi."

She accepted his reluctance and changed the subject. "My parents' ranch is in Davenport, near the Canadian border. I grew up working with my three brothers, often on horseback, roping, branding and moving cattle. Two of my three brothers were Marines. The middle one, Ed, was killed in Vietnam in sixty-eight."

"I'm sorry to hear that."

"We've never gotten over losing Ed. And my

parents..." Her head drooped, unable to finish her words.

He looked down at his plate, searching his mind for words. "For what it's worth, I'm sorry for your loss. From the way you mention his name, I would have liked to have known him."

"Thank you," she said in a soft voice. "I'm the only one of four kids who got a college scholarship," she continued. "I like the culture here on the coast, but I miss the rugged simplicity of ranch life and the drier climate. For now, at least, medicine is my calling. I never expected to be an ER specialist, but I love it."

"My turn to ask a question," he ventured after a pause.

"Fire away."

"I remember the first time we met. I brought a rape victim to the ER. Without saying anything you handed me your name and home phone number on a piece of paper within seconds of my walking in. How come?"

She shrugged. "I turned down every date offer for three years or so. Not one guy lit my fire. Then you came."

He looked at her, surprised.

"The moment I saw you, I was ready—I wanted you. Simple as that."

"My turn. Why did you call me the next day?"

"Same reason. Strong attraction. I felt flattered."

Rhonda glanced at her watch, a plain silver case

with white dial and brown leather strap. The kind people often associate with nurses.

"As you have to work tonight, we'll skip dessert. I have a surprise for you."

"Good thing, I'm stuffed."

She picked up the bill and reached for her purse. He snatched it from her.

"This is *my* treat," she protested.

"You're a girl, aren't' cha?" he countered as he fished a wad of cash from his pants pocket.

"Aye. As only *thou* knowest, m'lord," she said with a flirty grin and a wink.

He smiled ear-to-ear as he fished cash out of his wallet.

† † †

RHONDA'S HOME WAS a rustic one-story log cabin on two acres in the woods east of Redmond with a two-stall barn on a fenced pasture in the back. Once in the front door she put her arms around him and kissed him hard on the lips.

"Wait here and close your eyes," she said, love in her voice. "No peeking."

He heard her go out the back door and return in a moment. "You can look now."

Before him stood a handsome dog of Husky and German Shepherd lineage. His back, sides and head were black, a silver belly. His eyes were blue-green, and his tail curled up in a ring over his back, indicating Siberian Husky blood. Lean, deep-chested and large-boned, eighty pounds or more. Hitchcock extended his hand, palm down, by way of introduction. The dog sniffed, with caution at first, then lifted his eyes to Hitchcock's, wagged his tail and stepped toward him in acceptance.

"Where you live, surrounded by woods, you need a *real* dog," she said. "His name is Jamie. My cousin Karl owned a fenced construction equipment lot out in the east county. Thieves were going over the fence at night, robbing Karl blind. After he put Jamie in there, a couple guys who climbed over the fence at night got chewed up really bad. The thefts stopped."

"Why is he getting rid of him?"

"A former employee Karl fired for theft tried to break in one night. He thought because Jamie knew him, he could steal without trouble. He thought wrong. Jamie somehow knew he shouldn't be there. After much pain, suffering and hospital time he sued my cousin."

"No way! He got fired for theft, then goes back at night, breaks in, the dog does his job, the guy sues, the judge sides with him and orders the dog to be destroyed?"

"My thoughts too," Rhonda said. "The guy claimed he only went back for some belongings he forgot, and Jamie attacked him. Part of the settlement required Karl to put him down as a dangerous animal."

Hitchcock shook his head in disbelief. "What kind of judge would make a ruling like that?"

"One of the new breed of radical lawyers who are becoming judges nowadays. They hate cops and coddle criminals. In defiance of the judge, Karl gave Jamie to me on the sly, but I can't keep him. He's housebroken and his shots are up to date."

"Ah, you're giving me, a cop, an outlaw dog," he said with humor in his voice.

"I am," she giggled.

He beamed with pleasure as he took the leash and ran his hand over Jamie's haunches, shoulders and neck, working up to his head in a rough manner, assessing his strength. The dog's body felt like steel covered in skin and fur.

"How did you know what I needed, and how can I thank you, Rhonda?" he asked when they returned to his cabana.

She slipped her arm around his neck. They kissed more fully this time. "I knew because I am a woman," she said throatily as he held her in his arms. "As for thanking me, I'm sure you will come up with something acceptable to me, Mr. Hitchcock."

They rode back to his cabana in silence. He got out, holding Jamie on a leather leash. Rhonda wrapped her arms around his neck and kissed him fiercely on the lips, pressing her body into him. She patted his chest with her hand as she stepped back. His heart warmed as he watched Rhonda's Suburban disappear down the driveway. He knew she wanted marriage and babies, but the abortion and the Dear John letter from Ruby while he was in Vietnam sucked the last drop of emotional elasticity out of him. An emotional numbness like permafrost had taken its place.

Jamie leaned into his leg He gave the dog's head and body a rough rubbing with both hands. The house and grounds seemed to draw Jamie's attention. "Want to check the place out, eh? Go ahead, I'll follow," he said, waving his arm forward.

Jamie skirted the fenced swimming pool in the front lawn with his nose to the ground, then the main house, sniffing and marking the rhododendron flowerbeds by lifting a hind leg. His tail wagged and he glanced over his shoulder at Hitchcock when he reached the covered concrete patio which spanned the distance from the house kitchen to Hitchcock's cabana.

"Okay, Jamie, what else do you want to see?" He followed Jamie as he rounded the house to the back lawn, a sixty-foot span of emerald green, wet grass that stopped at the edge of a dense forest of tall evergreens, cedars and Douglas Firs, underbrush so thick the bare ground could not be seen.

Jamie quickly discovered a trail that began at the bedroom window at the back side of the cabana and trotted six feet ahead of Hitchcock, sniffing the ground, keeping an eye on his new master, stopping when Hitchcock stopped, moving when he moved.

Jamie's curled tail wagged joyfully as he followed

the trail into a dense stand of trees. It soon broadened to the width of a road and led through a tunnel of nearly leafless dogwood, alder and maple trees.

A thick blanket of fallen leaves covered the trail for a hundred yards. Hitchcock watched for overturned leaves, cigarette butts or wrapper, signs of foot traffic but found none. The trail ended at the tree line. The athletic field of Hyak Junior High lay forty yards beyond.

Hitchcock walked the trail back to the cabana, realizing for the first time the vulnerability of Doc's home to attack. He ruled out thieves using the long gravel road to get to the house from the paved street. It was easily eight hundred yards of straight, narrow road cut into the south slope of Wilburton Hill. No place to stash their car, no place to turn around.

A short, paved driveway lined with cedar trees curved uphill to the left at the end of the gravel road. It led to Doc's home and the cabana. *Anyone attacking Doc's place would have no choice but to leave their vehicle at the junior high and walk the trail to the back,* he concluded.
The rain resumed as they reached the cabana. He added raw hamburger to Jamie's dried kibble. As he watched him devour his first meal in his new home, he mentally asked himself, *If I were to do a hit on me, how would I do it?*

CHAPTER SIX
The Turning Point

THE RADICAL CHANGES sweeping over the country's cultural and moral landscape impacted the youth the most. The influx of mind-altering and addictive drugs blurred common values and commonly-held perceptions of right and wrong. Many of the Boomer Generation drifted aimlessly as result, living a day at a time, embracing lower standards and values than the generations before them.

Perhaps because of their insulated lifestyles, the heads of many financially successful, established families believed their kids would escape the destructive changes that embroiled so many others. Trouble with kids getting into crime or drugs was the bane of the lower income classes, they believed.

Certain families living in the wealthier neighborhoods of Bellevue and its suburbs along the east shore of Lake Washington, who had deep roots in business and the professions, fell into this category. They were the core of the community, hard workers, movers and shakers, job producers, supporters of charitable causes. For decades kids from these tight-knit families attended the best schools, took vacations in exotic places, won awards for academic and athletic achievements, and prospered after college as had their parents and grandparents.

"OLD TOWN" WAS the traditional name for the original town of Bellevue. The businesses and the properties along either side of Main Street were built in the '30s and '40s by families who founded and built the town into a city. Many of the shops still had the original hardwood floors. The original city hall, founded in 1952, was located at the end of Main Street where it became a Lake Washington Boulevard, a residential street that partly ran along the east shore of Lake Washington.

The police department was located in the basement of city hall back then. A light mounted on the outside wall of the station was turned on whenever a call came in. The on-duty officer would go to the call box mounted on a telephone pole at the other end of Main Street, and open the box with a key. The phone inside was connected to the station. The officer would write down the address and respond to the call.

As Bellevue grew, the quaintness of Old Town was preserved as an historic district.

North of Old Town was Bellevue's posh downtown core and surrounding neighborhoods, a mix of homes built in the '30s and '40s and newer, more stately abodes.

Scattered throughout the homes and businesses were a smattering of run-down, '40s vintage apartments, abandoned houses, sheds and a shanty motel consisting of nine separate cottages a half-mile north of the downtown core. Except for the motel, such places became hangout and hideout to a new class of small-time criminals–young dropouts, the children of well-to-do families, whose addiction to drugs and the influence of the "do your own thing" "live for today" subculture led to a life of petty crime, poverty and drifting.

Perhaps it was because of their more sheltered and privileged upbringing that these upper middle-class dropouts from the west side of town tended to be more civil than their counterparts east of the 405 freeway. Their criminal activity was limited to property crimes: burglary, shoplifting, and car prowling. They weren't inclined to taunt or sass the police. They didn't resist arrest or attempt to assault an officer. The few armed robberies and assaults on the west side of town were mostly the work of out-of-town people.

Drug and alcohol parties in abandoned homes, apartments, and on pleasure boats moored in Meydenbauer Bay lured new members to the subculture. The working public, who worked and ran the businesses and paid the taxes, chafed and complained as losses from car prowling and burglary mounted and little or nothing was done.

THOSE WHO ARE truly called to be policemen develop a feel for the pulse of their assigned beat. The rhythm of workplaces and neighborhoods and knowledge of the denizens through the seasons become so much a part of them that they *know* when something or someone is out of whack before anything has happened or been reported. It's what policing is about when the right chemistry is in place.

Officer Clive Brooks fit this description. He couldn't be a more natural fit for the ritzy west side if he tried. What he lacked in the bone-and-muscle department of his brother officers didn't deter him. He never failed to give a good account of himself in a fight.

Oddly enough, it helped Brooks with the citizens on his beat that he came across as a British army officer in a police uniform: slender and ramrod straight, fine-boned, wavy light-brown hair, chiseled-edge mustache, penetrating blue eyes, and old school manners.

As one destined from birth to wear a badge, Brooks took the people of his beat to heart. He had a sixth sense for trouble. Before anything happened that would draw the attention of the Department or the weekly town newspaper, Brooks knew when bad doings were afoot.

THE UNLIKELY STAR of the Patrol Division evolved

into a savvy uncle figure West Bellevue residents and businesspeople admired and trusted. His "Dutch Uncle Speech" to errant juveniles turned so many kids from the path of ruin he should have copyrighted it. Respect for Officer Brooks deepened to the extent that parents and teenagers alike told him, on terms of secrecy, about goings-on below the surface and who was doing what.

His fellow officers regarded him with brotherly fondness. Because he sometimes stuttered and talked more than he should, in typical cop humor, they gave him the affectionate nickname "Babbling Brooks."

Likeable, friendly and compassionate, Brooks won the trust and support of the people on his beat by being a faithful by-the-book cop who took the interests of the people on his beat to heart. By being attentive to detail and proactive to the point of tracking down juvenile runaways or recovering stolen property right after he took the initial report, he won widespread respect. Complaints against him were few and unfounded.

JUST PAST 11:00 p.m. on the last Sunday in September, a quiet Indian Summer evening of crisp, clear skies, the kind that carries sound as well as fog, Brooks sat in his patrol car on the north side of Main Street, facing the row of shops along the south side in Old Town. His window down, lights and motor off while writing a report, the sound of breaking glass startled him.

It came from across the street. Brooks could see

every one of the storefronts from his position—all appeared intact. The possible break-in had to be happening at the rear of one of them. He turned the radio volume down, keyed the mic and spoke softly. "Three Zero One, Radio. I hear glass breaking in the vicinity of 102nd and Main, in Old Town. Possible burglary in progress. Requesting backup."

LaPerle came on the air: *"I'm three blocks from you."*

Brooks: "The sounds came from one of the businesses along the south side of Main Street, east of 102nd. I'll be on foot, moving west behind the businesses. Drive slowly. I will see you."

Brooks's soft-sole shoes made no noise as he jogged across the street to the rear of the row of businesses. The shadowy parking lot, ringed on the other side by closed shops and sheds, seemed like an empty stage theater. He hunted in silence along the rear entrances of shops and diners.

He stopped frequently to listen and look, passing the back entrances of such town icons as Toy's Café and the Bellevue Barber Shop. He laid an open palm on the hoods of the few cars he passed. None were warm.

Moving in stop-and-start fashion from shadow to shadow, like a hunter in the forest, listening for more sounds to lead him to their source, Brooks crept westward, checking doors and windows.

At the last business, Lakeside Drugs, he spotted broken glass at the bottom of the short cement stairway.

He peeked around the corner.

The lights were out. The window to the left of the service door had been smashed inward and the door stood open. Scraping and prying sounds came from inside as LaPerle's patrol car came idling past the front.

Brooks drew his service revolver and crept up the steps to the landing as LaPerle's spotlight flooded the store with blazing light. A loud crash erupted from inside. A young white male carrying a backpack came running for the door.

"Stop. Police!" Brooks commanded.

The suspect ran wide, beyond Brooks's reach by a foot, leaped over all the steps, landed on both feet in the parking lot, still holding bags of loot in either hand and broke into an all-out run. Brooks took aim as the suspect sprinted across the lighted parking lot and headed for the shadows beyond.

"Police! You're under arrest! Stop or I'll shoot!" The suspect kept running. Brooks squeezed off a shot—*Blam!* The blast shattered the night calm.

The suspect kept running. Brooks aimed and fired again. *Blam!* The suspect staggered. Brooks watched, expecting him to fall, but he recovered and resumed his southbound flight, disappearing into the shadows. Brooks ran after him for a short distance, but the suspect had vanished.

LaPerle radioed "Shots fired" and sped to the back of the store where he spotted Brooks in the shadows, searching ahead with his flashlight. LaPerle got out of his cruiser, flashlight in hand and approached Brooks.

"What happened?"

Brooks stopped and pointed at the asphalt in front of him. "I knew it. My second shot got him," he said.

LaPerle looked where Brooks pointed. "Blood," he acknowledged. "What happened?"

"He's gotta be hiding around here somewhere. Let's keep looking."

They searched together along the narrow street that led into a neighborhood of two-story apartment buildings and old houses. LaPerle turned to Brooks when they found nothing. "Okay, Clive, what happened?"

Brooks sighed. "The suspect bolted past me when you shined your spotlight through the front window. He ran down 102nd, into the shadows. I ordered him to stop or I'd shoot, but he didn't. I fired twice. The second shot hit him. He staggered but kept running."

"You just made history in this town, Clive! As far as I know, no one has ever fired a shot at a suspect!" LaPerle exclaimed as he looked in the direction of the suspect's flight.

Darkness blanketed everything from the edge of the rear parking lot, about twenty feet from the back of the drugstore, to the entire length of the narrow residential street.

"Did you hear a car start up or a door slam?"

"Nope," Brooks replied.

"Breen's on his way, and the dicks will be here soon. Let's secure the scene before they arrive."

"We haven't checked the inside. We'd be embarrassed if there's a second suspect inside and the dicks find him instead of us," Brooks said with a mischievous grin.

LaPerle bowed with a smile and gestured to the door with an open hand. "Age before beauty–after you."

Brooks grinned at LaPerle's humor as he flipped the light switch. Guns at the ready, they searched the store, side by side, aisle by aisle, closet by closet. Brooks stood on a stool and raised several tiles of the suspended ceiling to check for suspects hiding there.

They found the cash register drawer busted open and empty. Two shelves in the back room had been swept clean. A short-handled sledgehammer and a chisel were on the floor next to the safe in the office.

"The suspect was here when you turned your spotlight on," Brooks told LaPerle. "He got as far as the second safe in a short time, where the cash is kept."

"Inside knowledge," LaPerle surmised, nodding.

"He busted open and cleaned out the safe for prescription drugs first. Then he went for the cash in the other safe. Gotta be a former employee," Brooks agreed.

"Past employee or a relative with a drug problem, most likely. He knew where the safes are but not the combinations," LaPerle said as he scanned the scattered contents on the shelves and the tools on the floor.

"The dicks will want to do their own processing, so let's secure the point of entry and exit."

"There's no alarm here, Clive?"

"This is Old Bellevue, Frenchie. The owners are old school, trusting. They think this part of town is surrounded by a white picket fence."

"It was, in a way, once upon a time…"

Brooks shook his head. "Not anymore."

Sergeant Breen arrived. Upon being briefed by Brooks, he detailed LaPerle and the District Two officer to search in the direction of the suspect's escape for any items he might have dropped and more blood trail.

Two detectives, a detective sergeant, and Frank Kilmer, the city photographer, arrived. The detectives joined the search for the suspect while Kilmer photographed the scene.

In the shadows about eighty feet from where Brooks fired his service revolver, LaPerle found more drops of fresh blood leading down the narrow residential street. The blood trail ended in less than ten feet, still in the middle of the street. *A suspect with a bullet wound would be more likely go right or left than straight ahead,* LaPerle reasoned. He glanced both ways. A small apartment complex on the right, an old house with detached one-car garage on the left. He checked the old house. Negative.

Detectives carrying flashlights joined the search, checking the apartment and other driveways for blood, inside every parked car and dumpster for someone hiding and felt every vehicle hood for a warm engine. None found.

Dispatchers called Overlake ER to ask if anyone came in with a bullet wound. Negative results. Records clerks phoned other area hospitals. Negative again. Detectives found numerous latent fingerprints at the scene, as would be expected in a store open to the public.

Though he got only a glimpse of the suspect in low light and the excitement of the moment, the closest distance between Brooks and the suspect had been five feet or less. He told the detectives at the scene, "I've arrested Michael Max Howard so many times I'm over ninety percent positive it was him."

† † †

COPS FROM BELLEVUE and its suburbs of Medina and Clyde Hill had been arresting Michael Howard for an ever- widening range of crimes since he was a juvenile. Now at the age of twenty, Howard had become a prominent figure in the under-realm of young, homegrown, drug-dependent petty thieves plaguing West Bellevue.

Though he came from an upper middle-class family, Howard lived as if he came from harsher origins; on the run from the law, using and dealing drugs in the basements of friends and girlfriends, in sheds, abandoned houses, or camps in the woods, stealing and leeching off friends for food and a place to stay, always in West Bellevue. With a police manhunt for him in full effect, and a stack of misdemeanor arrest warrants outstanding, Michael Howard, a Bellevue native all his life, vanished.

† † †

THE DOWNTOWN SHOOTING and the burglary made front page news in the weekly *Bellevue American*. An investigative article in the paper detailed the recent rise in downtown crime, citizen complaints to the police administration and its tepid response.

An avalanche of angry letters to the editor from downtown business owners appeared in the paper the following week. Claims of tepid police response to complaints of rising night-time commercial burglaries, vandalism and car prowls were cited.

Officer Clive Brooks deployed his network of confidants and informants he paid out of his own pocket, and his intimate knowledge of his beat to work. Acting on the inside information, he invaded the hideouts of small-time criminals in abandoned houses and newspaper shacks around the downtown. He made many arrests, including felonies, and seized drugs and recovered stolen goods.

Hoping the intensified patrols would result in Michael Howard's capture, Brooks contacted people at home at night for information. He met with parents as late as 10:00 p.m. without one complaint, such was his tenacity and reputation.

Between calls Brooks re-checked the places he had raided before and expanded his searches to camps in wooded lots and luxury watercraft docked at Meydenbauer Bay. He single-handedly rousted parties, made arrests for trespassing, outstanding warrants, drugs and minors in possession of alcohol.

Brooks often set Department records for arrests, especially felony arrests. But as much of a dent as he made in the crime problem in District One, he was only one of a handful of proactive officers.

A FIRESTORM OF criticism marked the next city council meeting a week later. Downtown business owners and managers as well as reporters from *The Bellevue American*, the town weekly newspaper, packed the council chambers. As expected, the front burner issue was the epidemic of property crimes being committed not only downtown but elsewhere in the city, though to a lesser extent.

As soon as the meeting was called to order, one business owner after another complained about the lack of police response to the increasing rate of burglaries, vandalism and thefts from their businesses. The Assistant City Manager addressed the council members and the crowd. "On behalf of our City Manager, who unfortunately could not attend tonight's meeting…" she began.

"Too afraid to face us, is he?" interrupted a business owner in the crowd.

Visibly flustered, the assistant stammered "Why, uh, no, of course not. Th-the CM knows what a poor job the police in this town are doing. That's why he's initiating a plan to–"

"Stop right there," said another shop owner, a balding, ruddy-face man who got to his feet. "We have it on good authority that the "CM" as you like to call him, has plans to discipline the officer who interrupted a burglary in Old Town for firing a shot at the burglar as he was escaping with drugs and cash. True or not?"

The assistant's jaw dropped, then she said, "Well, I-I can't say. I–"

"Tell your "CM" that Officer Brooks *better not* be persecuted for doing his job," the shop owner said, pointing his finger at the council members. "Our complaints *are not* against the police officers out there around the clock, seven days a week, or Chief Carter. Our complaints are against the City Manager's bias against the police department and the council's policies of not hiring enough officers to protect us and our property as the city grows." Murmurs of agreement rumbled through the crowd, and the shop owner sat down.

The city manager's assistant's voice stammered as

she said, "Oh, the CM has no animosity toward police."

"Don't you dare tell us that!" declared a fortyish woman with reddish blonde hair in a pony tail. "We hired you and your so-called CM, and we can fire you! We all read the paper. The city manager's snide comments like 'the police are but a necessary nuisance' are bad enough, but how about his latest gem: 'Cops should be disarmed.' Remarks like that encourage disrespect for our police and hurt our community."

The assistant city manager and her entourage walked out, red-faced, before the meeting was adjourned.

† † †

Two Nights Later
8:00 P.M.

THE RARE OCCURRENCE of Sergeant Breen smiling during shift briefing puzzled the squad. "Good news, boys," he said, "the Chief isn't taking this negative publicity laying down. We now have new portable radios and overtime pay for two-man foot patrol teams of officers willing to work overtime for the next three months to supplement downtown patrol car units."

Breen held up a blank sheet of lined paper on a clip board. "Here's the signup sheet. I grabbed it so you guys can have first crack at overtime and a chance to work on foot. Everybody from detectives, traffic, crime prevention and the station detail will be signing up. The new radios arrived this afternoon and are being charged. Foot patrols start tomorrow night. You snooze, you lose."

Hitchcock, eager to try foot patrol, and wanting overtime pay for the coming holidays, signed up first.

CHAPTER SEVEN
Blue Justice

THE NEWS BROKE on Friday, and an angry hush swept over each shift briefing when officers were told the full story. Officer Ronald Austin, of the rural Carnation Police Department took his life days after the prosecution declined to file charges against Jim McMinn and Crawford Beecham for what they did to him.

Home to the whistle-stop burgs of Fall City, Carnation, Snoqualmie, North Bend and Duvall, the Snoqualmie Valley in East King County consisted of small, family-run dairy farms in the lowlands, lumber mills and logging in the thick evergreen forests of the foothills. These deep woods havened outlaws and Ozark-style moonshine operations run by homegrown, deadly hillbillies like McMinn and Beecham.

The two stout, rough-hewn young woodsmen lived on the edge of the law and society as poachers of deer and elk, and as timber pirates who harvested fir and cedar from private woodlands, which they sold to small backwoods sawmills for cash. As brewers of moonshine in their private still, they sold their illegal 200-proof booze—known in rural areas as "everclear" or "white lightning"–to local bars, where the owners added it to labeled liquor bottles to cut their costs, unbeknownst to their customers.

McMinn and Beecham were of mixed Indian descent, and they lived as outlaws from an earlier century did. They shared the same cabin and the same women from the nearby Snoqualmie reservation. The duo lived by a code of looting and intimidation. Experienced barroom brawlers and hunters, each kept a rifle and a chainsaw in the cab of his pickup and packed a revolver on his belt.

They did not hide their scorn for cops. In particular, they loathed and mocked their local lawman, Ronny Austin, a man too short and slight of build to meet the standards of larger metropolitan police agencies.

Hitchcock came in on his night off for his first turn at foot patrol. His blood boiled when he listened to the circumstances that led to Austin's suicide. He remembered meeting Austin once when he picked up a prisoner from him at the Carnation Police station and the several minutes of friendly shoptalk. He didn't know until now that Austin was a fellow Army vet, an infantryman decorated for bravery during the 1968 Tet offensive.

The devil was in the details of how Austin died, and gruesome details they were. Months earlier, close to 3:00 a.m. on a Monday. McMinn and Beecham were parked in front of a closed tavern, facing the street, sitting in Beecham's pickup, drinking whiskey from the bottle with a girl from the reservation sitting between them. On routine patrol and the only officer on duty at the time, Officer Austin stopped to inquire of their business.

What happened next is a matter of conjecture, for neither Beecham nor McMinn, nor the girl would talk, and Austin was too traumatized to give a coherent account. But the town awoke the next morning to find Officer Austin naked from the waist down, beaten and bleeding, his arms secured with his own handcuffs around a telephone pole on the corner of the town's busiest intersection, his badge removed from his uniform shirt and pinned through the flesh of his exposed buttocks.

For hours, the citizens of Carnation drove by on their way to work, staring but not helping. School buses went by, kids yelling and jeering, forever breaking the spirit of a valiant man who had taken an oath to serve and protect them after risking his life to serve his country.

For Hitchcock and the other officers, what happened to Ronny Austin was a sobering reality check—even the law-abiding people they served and protected didn't like or respect them. Culturally and socially, cops were on their own.

IN THE LOUNGE of the Village Inn restaurant, located on the northwest corner of NE 8th Street and 104th Avenue, Bellevue's busiest intersection, McMinn and Beecham sat on bar stools drinking with another man, a small, refined, rodent with dainty hands and evil eyes, dressed in a dark suit.

McMinn shoved an envelope across the bar top to the shyster.

"Here's your fee, paid in full. Thanks for getting us out of this," McMinn said, as Beecham bobbed his head in agreement.

Smiling like a Cheshire cat, the scumbag lawyer quickly counted the bills before he slipped the envelope into his inside jacket pocket.

"Always glad to help anyone who hates cops the way I do," he said. As he knocked down the last of his drink and turned to leave, he gave parting advice to his clients: "Be careful in this town–cops here are pretty aggressive."

But McMinn and Beecham were feeling too cocky, too on top of the world to take advice. "We can handle 'em," they boasted between hoots of laughter.

Their campaign of witness intimidation paid off. Their reputations for retaliation and threats to burn down the houses of anyone who testified against them, the general community declined to refute their phony alibi. All charges were withdrawn due to "insufficient evidence."

McMinn and Beecham continued celebrating, gloating over their victory, clinking their glasses together, toasting Austin's death ever louder, to the discomfiture of other customers in the bar. As their glasses were refilled for the third time, two young couples entered and headed for a vacant table.

One of the women was especially attractive, and McMinn, feeling his firewater, turned on his barstool and whistled long and loud, followed by Indian war yelps, inviting her to sit on his lap as she passed by.

Her escort–a pasty-faced, slender youth wearing bell-bottom jeans, paisley-print shirt, Beatle hairstyle, and a pathetic, scraggly mustache–gulped as he protested. "Hey man, let's cool it."

"'Hey man, cool it?' Is that what you said, punk?" roared McMinn as he stepped off his barstool and stood mere inches from the girl's boyfriend. "Say that again and see how long you're on your feet! Then I'll take her for myself! Maybe my partner and I will both have her. Maybe we'll have her right in front of you. What'll you say about *that*, boy?"

Frozen with fear, knowing either of these human animals could wipe the floor with him with ease, the boyfriend stood speechless, his trembling visible under his paisley shirt.

The bartender broke in. "All right. You two are out

of here. Now, or I call the cops."

"Go ahead, call 'em!" Beecham snorted in a loud voice. "We beat the last cop who crossed us so bad he's dead now, so send 'em to us!" At that they both laughed and clinked their glasses together.

Sergeant Lane Baxter happened to be in the restaurant part, off duty, with his wife, Gloria, and overheard the ruckus in the bar. Being friends of the owner and the bartender, he decided to intervene before he was asked.

"Hey fellas, this is a nice place here. Let's go outside where we can talk about this."

Perhaps because of Baxter's obvious Indian heritage, McMinn and Beecham followed him outside.

In the open area of the front parking lot in the corner of an ell with the closed Marvel Morgan drugstore on the other side, the three men faced each other. Baxter offered to call them a cab.

"Nah, we're going back inside to take that young thing with us and beat the little white weasel with her if he tries to stop us," Beecham said. They turned to go back inside.

"No, wait," Baxter said. "Let me show you something."

Showing them his police badge, Baxter started to speak when Beecham slipped behind him. McMinn glared at him and said with menace in his voice, "I'm McMinn and my partner's Beecham. We beat little

Officer Ronny so bad he killed himself, and you're next!"

Beecham pulled Baxter's windbreaker down behind him, binding his arms, rendering him defenseless as McMinn slammed his fist into Baxter's stomach, forcing the wind out of his lungs. Doubled over, wheezing and gasping, a rain of loud, heavy fist blows pummeled Baxter's head and body.

As Baxter crumpled, his wife burst through the front door, running, her high heels clicking on the asphalt, screaming, arms flailing, desperate to save her man. "Stop! Oh God, Stop!"

McMinn spun around and punched her in the mouth, knocking her to the pavement, unable to get up. Seeing his wife down and bleeding, Baxter struggled to free his arms from his jacket and get back on his feet.

A crowd from the restaurant gathered on the sidewalk by the door. They cowered as they watched a helpless Baxter falling again under the merciless barrage of blows and kicks of two savage men. Not one person dared to help. Beecham paused from beating of Baxter and glared at the crowd.

"Which one of you lily-white cowards wants to be next?" Beecham roared. No one spoke up or intervened to save a fallen officer. They huddled together like terrified sheep, watching as Beecham and McMinn continued beating and kicking Baxter, who lay helpless on the asphalt, his groanings becoming fainter.

The night air carried the sounds of approaching sirens. Officer Mark Forbes, a body builder who had never been in a fight, arrived first. Eager to save Sergeant Baxter, Forbes bailed out of his patrol car. With one punch Beecham cratered Forbes's nose, causing him to buckle. Blood gushed. Forbes staggered. McMinn kicked his legs out from under him from behind and began kicking him in the ribs and head as soon as he hit the pavement.

Hitchcock and Wooten, the two-man foot patrol, arrived. McMinn seized Forbes's baton, whirled around and struck Wooten twice before he could draw his gun, snapping his collarbone. Wooten collapsed.

Joel Otis, the most admired and feared officer on the Bellevue PD, arrived in a cruiser and drew his baton as he faced McMinn, who began swinging Forbes's baton in a wild but controlled manner, chanting, war-dancing, taunting and challenging Otis, who headed straight at McMinn.

Taller, beefier, heavier-boned and perhaps stronger than Hitchcock, Beecham, surging with adrenalin, alcohol and bloodlust, uttering Indian war whoops, bent slightly from the waist and began a windmill with his fists as he faced Hitchcock.

Choosing his fists over his baton—exactly what the Brass tells officers not to do, the Department's newest officer, flipped his hat aside as he waded in, intentional destruction in every step, heading straight at Beecham.

Hitchcock's experience of over a hundred fights in Golden Gloves and Olympic-level boxing came into play. Bending at the waist, fists guarding his head, he bobbed and weaved between Beecham's wild punches untouched, closing in and landing a left jab as he pushed off with his right foot, putting his shoulder and the weight of his body behind the punch. Hitchcock's fist thudded against Beecham's nose, crushing it, rocking him back a step. Blood gushed right away.

The surprise on Beecham's face at the bone-breaking power of the punch and tasting blood changed to fear as Hitchcock closed in, almost forehead-to-forehead, and fired a right uppercut to Beecham's solar plexus, knocking the wind out of him and lifting him off his heels, followed by a left hook to the jaw that felled him like a tree. Hitchcock stood over Beecham as he rolled to one side, wheezing and bleeding, making a mighty effort to get up and fight back.

Hitchcock bent down and fired his right fist like a missile, striking the tip of Beecham's chin followed by a loud snap. Beecham collapsed again, unable to close his jaw. Bleeding from his mouth and nose, Beecham struggled to rise, but collapsed, utterly crushed in seconds.

Remembering McMinn, the second assailant, Hitchcock whirled to his right. He saw that McMinn, like Beecham, was on the pavement, retching and holding his stomach, his face and the top of his head covered in his own blood, while more blood bubbled from his open mouth with every breath. Otis was unscathed, of course, standing over McMinn, returning his baton to his belt ring.

The medic in Hitchcock checked on Gloria Baxter first, then Lane, who told him, "These are the two who beat Austin, the cop in Carnation. I heard them in the bar, bragging about causing his suicide before they attacked me."

Upon hearing this, Hitchcock strode back to Beecham, lying on the asphalt. He bent down, seized him by the front of his shirt and started to pull him to his feet, but stopped. They were done. The battle was over.

A two-man crew from Flintoff's Mortuary in Issaquah stood outside their hearse at Bob Osberg's Texaco across NE 8th from the scene, waiting for the signal to come in to attend to the injured.

Another siren wailed in the distance.

Surveying the scene—six bleeding bodies lying on the pavement—Hitchcock waved the crew in.

"We're former Army medics," he said, referring to himself and Otis. "Help us treat the injured."

They headed toward McMinn and Beecham.

"Not them! Treat the lady and the officers first," Otis barked.

The attendants stopped in their tracks. "But Officer, they're both bleeding," one of them said.

Otis pointed at Baxter and his wife, lying on the pavement. "See this lady and her husband? Those two did this to them and the two officers. They can wait!'

Lane and Gloria Baxter, Forbes and Wooten received first aid treatment, leaving McMinn and Beecham disabled and wallowing in their own blood. The swift destruction Hitchcock and Otis handed them, followed by being made to wait until their victims received care, crushed the power of their animality. Neither would be the same again.

CHAPTER EIGHT
Twists and Turns

SHOCKING NEWS AWAITED Hitchcock the following Monday at shift briefing–Colin Wilcox walked. Someone somehow sprung the hitman despite a state parole violation hold and pending new charges.

It happened over the weekend. An attorney representing Wilcox appeared before a District Court judge. Wilcox was released upon the posting of a cash bond of ten thousand dollars. Who posted the bond, no one seemed to know.

The release of Wilcox, a career criminal wanted on parole violation, a felon in possession of a firearm at the time of his arrest, forced Hitchcock to reassess his understanding of who really wields the power.

Hitchcock concluded the sacrifice of five-figure money through backroom deals to free Wilcox was done to keep prosecutors from offering him deals in exchange for information about who hired him and why.

Organized crime interests considered Eastgate's location on an interstate freeway at Seattle's doorstep to have strategic value for their operations.

Also, Eastgate offered less scrutiny and less likelihood of interference from the more experienced Seattle Police and federal agencies.

The closest experience Hitchcock had to the present situation was the communist insurgents who infiltrated peasant communities, the South Vietnamese army, known as ARVNs, and the police. He realized that most small to medium size police agencies like his were ill prepared to take on sophisticated challenges by organized crime elements.

He regarded the fact that no one on the Department had qualified with their service weapon for four years and counting because the powers-that-be closed the range as an indication of the City's closed-minded attitude toward crime becoming a reality. Thus, the Department, having no narcotics or criminal intelligence unit was helpless against experienced, well-financed criminal organizations.

It was a gloomy, depressing situation he was in. Nothing seemed tangible or real anymore. He felt alone in Eastgate, an environment he thought he knew—until reality pulled back its façade.

He radioed himself in service and drove straight to Charlie's Place. The owner's smile evaporated when Hitchcock shook his head and said, "We need to talk,

Wally."

✝ ✝ ✝

LANE AND GLORIA Baxter spent two days under observation at the hospital, where the docs watched for signs of brain injury. Lane, regarded by the rank-and-file as the most popular sergeant in the Patrol Division, sustained multiple contusions to his face, head and ribs, and would be off duty for some time. Lane's wife Gloria sustained head and neck injuries from being punched and hitting her head on the pavement. Lee Wooten had a fractured collarbone and a head concussion. Mark Forbes had a broken nose, battered and bruised ribs, back, and legs.

McMinn and Beecham were held on police holds at Harborview Hospital while recovering from severe injuries to their heads, internal organs, and broken bones. The prosecutor's office wasted no time filing multiple charges of felony assault on both men. News coverage fueled public outrage to the extent that the two outlaws were beyond the help of their scumbag attorney. For them, it would be many years of making license plates.

In another twist of justice, the rifle and revolver found in McMinn's pickup at the time of impound had been reported stolen in the burglary of a gun store in Carnation. The state lab identified the prints on each weapon as those of both McMinn and Beecham.

Hitchcock went further in his quest for justice for

Ron Austin. On the sly, he tipped off to Steve Miller, a cub reporter with the Bellevue paper, and the Feds, where he found McMinn and Beecham's moonshine operation in the woods, thus triggering a series of news stories and federal charges.

Thanks to the solid journalism of the Bellevue and Kirkland newspapers, the fallout from the fight was a public relations coup for the Department. Hitchcock and Otis declined interview requests from reporters, but the *Bellevue American* carried the full story anyway.

The series of articles written by Steve Miller began with McMinn and Beecham's campaign of intimidation of state's witnesses in the Ronny Austin incident and other crimes other agencies suspected them of.

Miller wrapped up the series by recapping Hitchcock's Golden Gloves career and his record on the 1964 Olympic boxing team, woven into the narrative was the history of Hitchcock and Otis growing up as neighbors, both later becoming Army medics at different times in Vietnam.

The combined stories of Brooks shooting at a fleeing burglar he caught in the act, and Otis and Hitchcock hospitalizing a pair of violent criminals who attacked civilians and officers created an afterglow of respect for the Department.

† † †

BROOKS WASN'T FOOLED by the public's newfound admiration for the police. He understood it was merely a fleeting window of opportunity to clean up his district. He knew the willingness of a fickle public to divulge information to the police wouldn't last long.

Making the most of a rare opportunity, Brooks put his knowledge and photographic memory to work. His briefcase typically over-flowed with old stolen car lists, called "hot sheets," and copies of the *Western States Crime Conference* bulletins which contained reports of the movements and methods of professional shoplifting rings, safecrackers, burglary teams and armed robbery gangs roaming the West.

The rate of burglaries and car prowls plunged as a result of Brooks's proactive work and the many on-view arrests made by the downtown foot patrols. These developments, together with other publicized feats of the Patrol Division got Chief Carter off the political hot seat and temporarily thwarted the secret plans of the Department's detractors.

But not everyone was satisfied with the outcome.

IF BEECHAM HAD attacked Hitchcock with a baton or any weapon, as McMinn did to Otis, Hitchcock would have shot him dead on the spot.

Under state law and Department policy, Otis could have shot McMinn when he attacked him with a baton. McMinn, Hitchcock believed, more than Beecham, deserved to pay with his life not only for what he did to Austin, but for trying to club Otis. Killing him would have sent the strongest possible warning to the criminal community about attacking Bellevue officers.

Hitchcock believed Otis didn't shoot McMinn because of the Brass and the City Manager's attitudes regarding police officers using deadly force.

For years officers feared that supervisors above the rank of sergeant would side with complaining citizens without listening to both sides of the issue. Some officers believed their superiors were intimidated by anyone with a college education.

Brooks broke the ice when he shot at a fleeing burglar. Officers expected the Brass to throw him to the wolves, but the town's movers and shakers stood by him publicly, hailing him as a cop with guts, saving him from political consequences for firing his weapon.

ANOTHER CRISIS ON the Department's horizon was the soon-coming changing of the guard. Chief Sean Carter would announce his retirement any day. An affable type everyone liked, an able cop in his day, Carter was a husky, good-natured, red-headed New York Irishman. It was no secret that he looked forward to retiring to his New York City roots. In the new climate of uncertainty and unrest, the troops, who liked and respected Carter, regarded him as too passive and too close to retirement to take the political risks necessary to meet the new demands on the Department.

To a man, Patrol officers wanted Captain Erik

Delstra as their next chief. Delstra, a smart, bold, take-no-prisoners type some officers likened to General George Patton of WWII fame.

"We'd have a *real* department, like Seattle, if we had Delstra as our Chief," the troops said among themselves at their almost daily post-shift drinking sessions. They believed the chances of Delstra becoming Chief to be slim to none. In the current environment of political timidity and cultural passivity, city decision makers feared controversy too much to take a chance on a bold, outspoken leader like Delstra. The city leaders were already scouting nationwide for Carter's replacement.

† † †

THE QUIET IN District Six allowed Hitchcock time to assess the Wilcox situation further. Despite high bail and state holds, someone had the cash and the influence to spring Wilcox out of jail. It forced him to understand that real power wasn't held by citizens or elected leaders, but by the rich and powerful in the shadows.

The weather was cool and clear. Sitting in his cruiser in the empty parking lot of the Safeway store, facing the freeway, Hitchcock felt a dread come over him that he couldn't shake. Out of the blue he prayed: "God, I became a cop instead of a doctor to help people, and my people are dying from drugs. I don't know how to fight this. If You're real, please point me in the right direction."

He resumed patrol, amazed at himself for talking to

God–something he hadn't done since his father died.

The radio was quiet as he re-checked the buildings and the equipment yards located below the north frontage road. Returning to Eastgate, he checked the front and back of The Great Wall. No cars. Inside it was locked up, lights out. Charlie's Place and The Wagon Wheel closed early.

Past midnight, he crossed the freeway overpass and spotted a man sitting alone in a black, late-model Mercedes, headlights off, in the Albertson's parking lot, facing the freeway.

The stores, including Albertson's had been closed for hours and the parking lot was empty except for this Mercedes, which was parked alongside the store, not out in front, which struck Hitchcock as odd.

He drove past the Albertson store, out of sight of the Mercedes, then u-turned, entering the parking lot, headlights off. From a distance of thirty yards behind and off to the left of the Mercedes, Hitchcock focused his binoculars on the interior.

The driver was watching the Bellevue Airfield on the other side of the freeway with binoculars. The airfield was closed and the runway lights were off, as always after business hours.

He shifted his focus to the airport. To his surprise, the freeway lights were so close to the airfield that they illuminated the runway remarkably well.

The airfield was empty. As he wondered what the

man in the Mercedes was doing here, a small plane dropped out of the night blackness and landed on the runway. The headlights of a car waiting beside a darkened hangar flashed twice, then it approached the plane. He recognized its outline as that of a new model Mustang. Two men got out and faced the plane. One of the men held a briefcase.

Hitchcock's heart quickened when he saw two men get out of the plane and face the men from the Mustang. One of them also held a metal briefcase. The posture of the four men was tense, combat ready, their feet shoulder width apart.

A man from the plane set a briefcase on the pavement and stepped back. A man from the Mustang took up the case, and the other man from the Mustang handed a bulky item that looked like a briefcase to the man from the plane, who appeared to inspect the contents. Seconds later the Mustang left and the plane took to the air.

Hitchcock sat, unbelieving, his heart racing. He had just witnessed the transfer phase of a smuggling operation. *The man in the Mercedes has to be involved or at least has guilty knowledge.* He ran the plate number. No warrants on the registered owner, North Seattle address.

He pulled up behind the Mercedes with his headlights still off and approached along the passenger side, looking inside to locate the man's hands.

His hand on the grip of his service revolver, he rapped his knuckles lightly on the front passenger window, staying back far enough to force the driver to turn his head to see who it was.

Instead of being startled, the driver smiled as he powered the window down. *This guy is too smooth.* Hitchcock kept his eyes on the man's hands as he turned on his stuttering dumb cop act.

"Uh, excuse me, sir. I sure am sorry to be bothering you like this, but I'm just making sure you're all right and, uh, well, I see that you are. Uh, and, pardon my saying so, sir, but wow, you sure got some car here. Are you, uh, waiting for someone getting off work at the store here, mebbe?"

Another too-smooth smile. "Well, hello, officer. I'm just fine, thanks. I just came here to watch planes land at night. Interested in flying myself. No private airports near me, so I came here to watch. Night landings are tricky, and they fascinate me. Thought I'd watch and learn."

The man fit the Mercedes; a well-groomed executive type, early forties, polished manners, standard haircut, expensive leather jacket over a cashmere sweater. His smooth over-politeness and knowing to keep his hands in sight without being told added to Hitchcock's suspicions.

"No problem, sir. Learning at every opportunity is the way to go, I always say. Well, uh, we sure do got us some dandy wonderful weather tonight to be out, sir. Sure do wish I could do the same instead of working tonight." Hitchcock glanced around the Mercedes interior, then shook his head in admiration. "If you don't mind my saying so, sir, this sure is a nice car you have here. Is it yours?"

Another oily smile. "Yes, thank you, it is."

"Would you show me your ID and registration, please?"

The man kept his oily smile intact as he said, "Why, yes, of course. I must say, officer, your thoroughness certainly makes me feel safe."

"Why, thank you, sir! You just made my whole night worthwhile," Hitchcock gushed, still acting the oaf as his fingertips touched the grip of his revolver when the man's right hand disappeared from the steering wheel. A moment later he came up holding his wallet and handed his driver's license to Hitchcock. Then he opened his glove compartment and handed him the car registration.

The address on his driver's license matched the registration for the Mercedes. Hitchcock already knew the man was clear of warrants, but he had lied—there were two private airfields in Seattle closer to his address than Bellevue. *He was waiting for the plane to arrive! How did he know there would be a night landing here tonight and at this time?*

As the Mercedes left, and Hitchcock noted the

vehicle and driver information, and a description of what he saw at the airfield and his suspicions about the activity on a Field Interview Report form and in his field notebook.

He re-patrolled the business district aggressively, checking cars parked in businesses and public parking areas. He checked behind The Great Wall. It had been closed all night, but earlier he had noticed lights on in the back, not the front dining area. Two cars, neither belonging to Juju, had been parked at the rear. Wondering what was afoot, he had copied the plate numbers and checked the back door. He jiggled the back door knob. Locked.

Now, at 1:00 a.m., both cars were gone and the lights were out. For most legitimate businesses, this would be the time the owners and the managers do inventory. The strange hours and activities at The Great Wall were a growing puzzle for which he had few pieces.

He changed location to write up his notes. The license plates of the strange cars he saw earlier. were registered to owners with Asian surnames Hitchcock didn't recognize and Seattle addresses. He added the details to his notebook and resumed patrol.

A WEEK LATER, he began his shift by changing his routine. Out of instinct he headed for Juju's place at 8:00 p.m. It made him suspicious to see it closed for the second night in a row on a week-night. No cars front or back.

He was called away to back up Walker on a family beef call in Lake Hills. As soon as they cleared, they rolled to a disturbance call to Charlie's Place.

Two men argued over the same attractive blonde, middle age woman he noticed at Charlie's the night he arrested Colin Wilcox. It surprised Hitchcock that the woman went along with the men agreeing to flip a coin to see which of them would leave with her.

As midnight approached, the influx of calls dropped. The late-night bowling league crowd drifted over from Sunset Lanes to The Wagon Wheel for drinks before going home. Hitchcock went in to have a look around. A young bartender with a cherubic face and a full head of red hair named Ralph chatted with two women sitting at the bar. Couples wearing bright colored, silky bowling league shirts sat drinking at three tables.

A new barmaid, a pretty, shapely brunette, buxom, dressed in a long-sleeved white blouse and black skirt, smiled as if she knew him. Intrigued, Hitchcock smiled back.

The almost zero noise of light freeway traffic as he left the bar enabled him to hear the droning of an engine above him.

Out of the black sky he made out the red and green lights of a small plane descending toward the airport. He sprinted to his patrol car. Precious seconds were lost unlocking the driver door. His heart raced as he sped to the airfield.

The plane rose into the night as he arrived. A new black Mustang, two men on board, passed him on their way out as he entered. Hitchcock tried to turn around in time to stop it. By the time he reached the exit, it was gone. He noted the details of the second night landing in his notebook and wrote up an internal memo for the detectives.

AFTER THE BARS closed and the streets were clear, Hitchcock met Walker at the Eastside Disposal transfer site below the frontage road and the freeway to Seattle. "Haven't fired my weapon since we did this last time," Walker chuckled as he swapped duty ammo from his revolver with practice loads.

"The criminal element will breathe a sigh of relief to know that, no doubt," Hitchcock joked.

"Truth be told," Walker went on as he holstered his gun and filled his pants pocket with more practice ammo, "I prefer to shoot here, 'specially in the dark, than that hokey excuse for a range the commies on the city council took from us. Here we got live targets that move, and besides, most gunfights happen at night."

"Good point, Ira."

Leaving their windows down and the volume on their radios turned up, they scaled the chain link fence and dropped onto a large, smooth concrete pad on the other side. Thirty feet across from them were mountains of wet garbage that had been piled under an open-sided metal roof.

"I'll go first," LaPerle said.

Hitchcock aimed his flashlight at the pile of garbage. Within seconds, a large rat appeared, then another. The rats both stopped for a moment in the beam of light. Walker drew and fired one round. The bullet went wide.

Under the beam of Walker's flashlight Hitchcock fired at the next rat, and thus they dueled, keeping score on rats killed versus missed. By the time they had each fired six rounds, they heard Dispatch calling: *Three Zero Six, and Three Zero Eight, residents in the Woodridge area are again reporting what sounds like shots fired in the vicinity of Richards Road near the freeway.*

They scrambled over the fence to their cruisers. Hitchcock smirked as he keyed the mic. "Three Zero Six is en route, Radio."

Walker radioed: *"In the area now—don't hear anything."*

"10-4. Both units, remain in the area. Still getting calls.

"Received," Walker replied, shaking with laughter as he reloaded his gun with duty ammo.

"You're shooting is off, Ira," Hitchcock said "Woman-trouble can distract a man, leading to deadly mistakes. Set your problems aside when you come to work. Women have their place, but in our line of work, they must be kept in place when we're on duty."

Walker lit a cigarette. "Don't I know it," he said, exhaling a plume of smoke. "So how should I train?"

"Do slow draws from the holster with your gun unloaded. Take the time to grip your gun properly, using both hands and bring the weapon up to eye level while keeping your body straight. Doing this on a daily basis builds muscle memory. If you're wounded in a fight for your life, your body will continue to fight on its own. Repeat this empty gun drill twenty-five times a day, at home before every shift. Speed will come on its own."

"No ammo?"

Hitchcock shook his head. "If you do this daily, you only need to practice with live ammo once a week. I'll spring for an extra box of Frenchie's practice handloads when mine are ready. You should have it day after tomorrow."

"You're a buddy, Roger."

HE REMEMBERED ALLIE. He'd yet to run the plate of her ex-husband's car or the phone number for the mysterious Jim Reynolds.

Clearing the "shots fired" call after another ten minutes, he called Records from a pay phone. Patty answered. He gave her the license plate of Allie's ex-husband's Mercedes, and the name and phone number of Jim Reynolds.

Patty wanted to chat. "Hey, Roger, we were

impressed with the way you and Otis put those two thugs down at the Village Inn the other night. Must have been a scene like in the movies. The word is they're both still at Harborview, all busted up. I understand that McMinn, the guy who fought with Otis, may have permanent brain damage. Beecham's jaw is wired shut and he's on a liquid diet."

"They got off lucky," Hitchcock said.

Patty chuckled. "We read in the paper about your Golden Gloves career—seven first place trophies and you were on the '64 Olympics boxing team. None of us here were aware of your background."

"I don't talk about it much."

"I read that your dad boxed, too."

"He took it further than I did. Dad fought semi-pro to pay his medical school costs."

"So, your dad taught you?"

"Initially, yes."

"Changing the subject, the other night when you guys were on that chase, Sergeant Breen paced the floor nonstop, chain-smoking, his face was so blood-red we feared he'd have a heart attack when your radio 'went down.'"

"I can imagine what Jack went through, everything was on the line for all of us, but he stood by us when others would've written us up," he replied.

"He sure did. Anyway, I'll have the info in your inbox before end of shift."

AFTER 4:00 A.M. he left the station for Allie's apartment. He waited across the street where he could keep an eye on her Toyota in the parking lot. While he waited, he read the information Patty left for him, and let out a low whistle.

The Mercedes Allie's ex drove was registered to a high-profile, prominent Seattle family which owns several blocks of downtown Seattle, where an office building bore the family name. Broadmoor address, the most exclusive guarded and gated neighborhood in Seattle. The contrast between her ex-husband's wealth and Allie's humble circumstances raised questions in his mind.

The strange case of Jim Reynolds needed attention. The mystery deepened when he learned Reynolds had given Allie an unlisted phone number. The phone company required a court order or at least an "administrative subpoena" from a detective before they could release subscriber name and address.

He didn't know any of the detectives well enough to ask for a favor, and he wanted to know more about Allie and the guy calling himself Jim Reynolds before he submitted a formal report. When he tried a search on his own, he found there were too many Jim Reynolds in the greater metropolitan area to sort through.

A few minutes after 5:00 a.m. an attractive middle-aged woman, blonde hair in curlers, arrived in an older sedan. As she got out of her car and went up the stairs, Hitchcock noticed her remarkable resemblance to Allie. Using a key, she entered Allie's apartment without knocking.

Allie emerged minutes later, wearing a white waitress dress under a blue ski parka.

Seeing her again brought a smile to his face. Even in her plain white waitress dress and bulky ski parka, she radiated femininity. He shook his head. *Ah! Stick to the objectives—see if "Jim Reynolds" or anyone else follows her to the Pancake Corral, or is already there, waiting for her.* He followed her to work

Satisfied no one else followed her or was waiting for her when she arrived, Hitchcock decided to be her first customer of the day. She smiled with delight when he walked in. "Fancy seeing you here this early," she said.

"Just happened to be in the neighborhood," he fibbed as he settled into a booth.

"Any more info on or from your ex?"

Allie smiled at him as she poured his coffee.

CHAPTER NINE
Living on the Edge

WITH A HITMAN at large, Captain Holland called an emergency meeting of his detectives. "Colin Wilcox jumped bail," he announced. "He didn't show for his pre-trial hearing; his uncle's car is still in impound. We have a hitman on the loose, to find him, let's review what we have."

"There's a cigar box full of cash receipts in evidence," Sergeant Jurgens said. "Hitchcock found it under the driver seat."

"Use 'em to chart his movements and show his mugshot to everyone he contacted," Holland said.

"We won't have to look too hard–the bounty hunters will be after him," Detective Meyn said.

"We found a list of phone numbers in Wilcox's glove box. The phone company is reversing them. Whoever hired him might be on the list," was Detective

Small's contribution.

Captain Holland turned again to Sergeant Jurgens. "What's the status on the lab reports and the gun?"

"The reports came in yesterday. Wilcox's prints were on the Browning Hi-Power pistol, as well as both magazines," Jurgens said. "The gun isn't listed as stolen. Tracing it from the factory will take the Bureau of Alcohol, Tobacco and Firearms, a couple more weeks."

"Since we have no further need of the car, assign somebody to call Wilcox's uncle about picking it up, and ask if he's had any contact with his nephew," Captain Holland told Jurgens.

"Williams will handle it," Jurgens replied.

"Next, notify Wally Evans, the owner of Charlie's Place that Wilcox is out, and we have no idea where he is."

"Hitchcock already did that on his own time, Captain," Jurgens said.

"Okay, so Patrol knows Wilcox is out, what else are they doing?"

"They're keeping Wally Evans's home on a Patrol Watch until further notice," Sergeant Jurgens replied.

THE COURT ISSUED a no-bail arrest warrant for Wilcox. The detectives filed an additional charge of felon in possession of a firearm on the same day. Wilcox's uncle picked up his car. Detective Small's investigation of the subscribers of the phone numbers on the list found in the car was a dead end. With no other leads, everyone in the division returned to other cases.

It didn't take long for the normal flow of calls and another spike in drug overdose cases and seizures of marijuana and cocaine to overshadow the Colin Wilcox matter. With evidence in place and charges filed, Hitchcock too, returned his attention to routine patrol, but with a new wariness.

Wilcox being at large made him feel vulnerable. For the first time since Vietnam, he constantly looked over his shoulder, checking his rear view mirror to see if anyone followed him, hesitating before passing through a doorway, going nowhere unarmed.

Any doubt that the chance arrest of Wilcox thwarted a professionally planned mission aimed at Charlie's Place was erased, only the purpose remained a mystery. Hitchcock believed even Wilcox probably didn't know *why* he was there, only *what* he was supposed to do.

On his next day off, Hitchcock bought a .38 double-barrel derringer as a hideout gun at Warshall's Sporting Goods in downtown Seattle. Egbert "Eggs" Voigt, the leather craftsman in Issaquah who made the Department's leather gear, made an inside-the-waistband holster for the small, flat-sided two-shooter.

THE WILCOX INCIDENT haunted Hitchcock. He went to Charlie's Place off duty where he found Wally tending bar.

"We need to talk again," he said.

"That we do," Wally replied. He told his barmaid to take over and pointed to the back. "My office."

Door closed, Wally's massive wooden desk between them, covered with envelopes and stacks of papers. Hitchcock got right to the point. "What do you think Wilcox came here to do?" he asked.

Wally slowly shook his massive head. "I've hardly slept since it happened. Robbery is my only guess, but why wouldn't he wait until just before closing? There'd be fewer people and more cash by then."

"We've ruled out robbery. I can't divulge the reasons. But somebody behind him had the juice to bail him out in spite of state holds on him for parole violation and being a felon in possession of a firearm. Turns out that Wilcox is a well-known hitman."

Wally stared at Hitchcock. "The hell you say?"

"You're from Chicago, so I'm asking–do you have any enemies who would want have you to rubbed out?"

Wally shrugged his shoulders and shook his head in dismay. "That can't be why Wilcox came here. I've never crossed anyone in my life."

"What brought you out here from Chicago?"

"A better life," Wally said matter-of-factly. "We were living on the South Side, where I grew up. Our kids were nearly school age. Crime had worsened in my old neighborhood since I was a kid, same story at the schools. Barbara and I wanted schools where there are no gangs, neighborhoods where it's safe to walk the dog at night. Barbara had been out here before, so—"

"That's good enough for me, Wally," Hitchcock cut in. "But it doesn't explain Wilcox coming here two nights in a row, armed and disguised."

"No, it doesn't. What can I do to protect myself, my family—this place?"

"Our Crime Prevention Unit has portable alarms. Varda alarms, they're called. They can put one in your home and another one here, so if there's an emergency you just hit a button and the station dispatchers automatically sends two units without you having to make the call, then they call you."

"I appreciate it, Roger, I really do," Wally said.

"Now, let's come up with some code words for you and your employees to use in case of emergency when they call the station or when an officer walks in unawares during an emergency situation."

THE ARMY TAUGHT Hitchcock that every mission ends when either the objective has been accomplished, or the point of diminishing returns renders further efforts a waste of time. Neither ending had yet been realized in the Wilcox matter, but the leads were dwindling.

The missions he went on in Vietnam, searching for the enemy in a foreign country, culture and climate were successful when the Army developed informants among the local populace by providing medical care, food, and protection from Viet Cong raids. Grateful people reciprocated by giving vital information regarding enemy locations and plans.

The strategy won battles and saved lives. If he could duplicate what the Army did—develop his own network of informants, or even one—he could deal a lethal blow to those profiting from drug trafficking. The catch was how to go about it in a civilian setting.

† † †

HITCHCOCK COULDN'T HANDLE cold weather well after three years of living in warm sunshine every day. Now, he wore lined leather gloves and his heavy uniform coat when a dry cold snap interrupted the November rains and caused the usual cloud cover to freeze and fall down. Evening temperatures in the mid-twenties meant icy roads, keeping most people inside, but not the police.

At 8:20 p.m. he drove past The Great Wall. It was closed, which he attributed to the weather this time. No cars were there, front or back. Nevertheless, he peeked inside, aiming his flashlight beam through the windows. Nothing.

At a few minutes past 10:00 p.m., while on a traffic stop on the frontage road in front of The Great Wall, which was still closed, Hitchcock heard, then saw, a Harley chopper with ape hanger handlebars, deafening exhaust, ridden by a bearded biker wearing dark sunglasses, roar into view from behind The Great Wall.

The biker taunted Hitchcock by gunning the throttle, making as much noise as he could as he passed within a foot of Hitchcock, then roared out of sight.

Remembering that The Great Wall had been closed all night, seeing the front windows were still dark, Hitchcock checked the back again as soon as he cleared the traffic stop.

Now, two late model luxury sedans he didn't recognize and Juju's Cadillac El Dorado were parked in the back. All three cars had warm hoods. Lights were on in the back only. He tried the door. Locked.

Hearing his radio crackling, he returned to his cruiser. *Assist the State Patrol in a multiple car, injury accident on eastbound Highway 10, east of the Eastgate overpass until they arrive. Code Three.*

He arrived in seconds behind a full-sized Mercury sedan nose-first on the gravel median that had a bundle of long steel reinforcing rods projecting through its rear window.

Standing at the driver door of the sedan was a middle age man dressed in worn jeans, a dark wool shirt with the tails out, his hands in his pockets. He was leaning forward, talking to the driver.

Hitchcock as he stepped out of his cruiser. He saw the bundle of steel reinforcing rods extended past the truck bed by ten feet or more, and had pierced the driver side of the Mercury sedan windshield behind the truck.

"I'm the truck driver, officer, and I'm not hurt," the man said. He gestured to the driver of the Mercury. "This fella needs help, though."

The man in the driver seat of the Mercury, a thin, balding man in his fifties, was conscious but dazed. Blood from a gash in his forehead ran down his face. "What happened to you, sir?"

A vacant stare at Hitchcock, but no reply. He smelled alcohol on the driver's breath as he checked the man's pulse and pupils with his flashlight.

"You don't seem to have a concussion sir," Hitchcock told him. "Your pupils are even, which is good. Take it easy while I get my first aid kit."

He heard the sound of an animal whimpering in pain as he bandaged the driver's head wound. A Doberman puppy was on the back seat, its head and chest bleeding. *I need an ambulance and a tow truck, a state trooper, and now I need a veterinarian.*

Hitchcock returned to the truck driver, still standing by the Mercury, hands in his jeans pockets, "What happened, sir?"

"The punk on the Harley came from out of nowhere and cut me off at a high rate of speed," he shrugged. "He'd be dead if I didn't brake and swerve as hard as I did."

"The guy on the Harley?"

"Yeah, sent him and chopper flyin' like he was shot out of a cannon," the trucker said, nodding at the median.

On the gravel median a few yards ahead of the flatbed truck and the Mercury sedan laid the same biker Hitchcock had seen moments earlier. On his back, legs spread. The frame and front wheel of his motorcycle next to him were mangled.

"Hey, buddy. You all right? You hurt?" Hitchcock asked.

The biker had no apparent injuries. He lifted his head, looked at Hitchcock and moved his arms and legs. Hitchcock noted lightning bars tattooed on his neck. His eyes widened and his face contorted with hostility when he saw Hitchcock standing over him.

"Get outta here, Bellevue pig!" he screamed, followed by a stream of obscenities.

"Easy now. The State Patrol and an ambulance are on their way. I'm just asking if you're injured and what happened."

The biker let loose another torrent of obscene curses at Hitchcock, some he hadn't heard since the Army, plus a few that were new to his ears.

A young state trooper, trim and proper, arrived. The ambulance took the injured driver of the car to the ER.

Hitchcock helped the trooper restrain the biker when they stood him up. His delirium and smelling of alcohol necessitated taking him to Overlake Hospital in handcuffs for an involuntary blood draw.

The hearse from Flintoff's arrived from Issaquah, treated the injured driver of the Mercury and transported him to the Overlake ER.

The Doberman puppy on the back seat of the mercury sedan died before a veterinarian arrived.

Hitchcock met the trooper at the Overlake ER, where the biker was strapped on a gurney, ranting incoherently, struggling to break free of the restraints. The results of the involuntary blood draw were expected momentarily.

A hospital security guard appeared.

"Are you Officer Hitchcock?"

He nodded.

"There's a call holding for you at our front desk."

He followed the guard down the corridor and picked up the phone. *"It's Wayne, in Dispatch, Roger. Can you break free? Unidentified caller reports cocaine sales going on inside the bar at The Wagon Wheel. Suspect's name is Jimmy, white male, late twenties, blue dress shirt, tie, dark slacks. Baggies of dope in his front pants pocket."*

"On my way."

CHAPTER TEN
A Fight, and The Pretty Bar Maid

IN A BOOTH by the front window in the dim realm of The Wagon Wheel lounge sat Frank Durham, a leather-faced, decorated, retired Marine in his forties. A young, svelte brunette beauty sat across from him. The usual crowd of late-night league bowlers greeted and cheered the veteran of Iwo Jima and Korea as they filed in for their traditional nightcap before going home.

Frank may have been past his prime, but the uniforms of his youth still fit him, for he kept himself fit since he retired eleven years ago. As he started his second glass of Johnny Walker Red, the young beauty looked at him.

"Dad, I want to go," she said softly.

"I just started my drink—can't you wait a few?"

She indicated the bar with her eyes. "That man over there keeps ogling me."

Frank turned his head to a man sitting at the bar,

staring at them. "Who, him? Is he bothering you, Renee?"

"Yes. Please, Dad—no trouble. Remember what the doctor said. Let's leave now."

"You drive," he said, handing her the keys.

That man was Jimmy Combs, late twenties, a weasel-faced, twice divorced, deadbeat father of four, all-around bar fly, car salesman, gym rat and occasional drug dealer.

Tonight, Jimmy was feeling cocksure of himself. After several sales trips to the men's room with other men, his wallet bulged with cash. Now, after his fourth beer, his caution and inhibitions were so lowered that he sold another baggie of white powder in the bar where others could see him.

Jimmy had pestered another brunette for a date earlier in the evening—the alluring new barmaid. When she told him to bug off, he turned his attention to the new arrival, the young fox sitting in a booth across the table from a much older man.

The more Jimmy drank, the more he leered at her. When she touched the old man's hand, Jimmy left his barstool, cocky and smirking, as he swaggered toward the couple.

"How about a *young* man, tonight, foxy lady?" Jimmy said. "A real man who isn't washed up like this geezer."

A hush fell over the crowd when Frank knocked his

glass over as he bounded out of the booth. He stood, arms at his sides, fists clenched.

Jimmy came within inches of Frank's face, mocking him with a sneer. He glanced down and stepped on Frank's foot. Frank slammed the heel of his palm into Jimmy's chest, shoving him back.

Did you see that, everybody?" Jimmy crowed. "The old man here pushed me. I say he needs a lesson in manners." He slammed his palm into Frank's chest, sneering.

Frank knew he didn't have the strength or the speed he did when he was his opponent's age, but he had experience in his favor. He had killed men in combat in the Pacific and in Korea. Jimmy was a sick joke to him. He provoked his opponent's anger with a chuckle. "You look like you work out in a gym, in front of a mirror, in a pink bikini," he said. The sounds of snickering came from the onlookers who gathered.

Jimmy's smile evaporated and his face reddened. He took a step back and planted his feet shoulder-width apart. "We'll see who's who, old man. Take your best shot."

Ralph the bartender stepped in between the two, clutching an aluminum kid-size baseball bat in one hand. "Take the fight outside or I call the cops," he said, glaring at Jimmy.

The lounge emptied out quickly as the crowd followed the fighters to the parking lot.

A crowd of excited customers and bowlers encircled the old veteran, and the young hyena right outside the lounge window. They faced each other across an open space of twenty feet, staring at each other like boxers waiting for the bell to ring.

Renee cringed when a woman in her mid-thirties, brown hair in a ponytail raised a handful of cash in the air. "I'm betting three to one on Frank to be the last man standing! Who's game tonight?"

Sounds of bloodlust filled the air as onlookers speculated about the fighters. Bets were placed and cash changed hands. The excited murmuring for the fight to begin became a crescendo as the crowd grew in size and the fighters stared at each other.

A couple of the older men acted as Frank's seconds, rubbing his shoulders, whispering advice into his ear.

"Last chance, old man. I'll let you off with an apology," Jimmy jeered.

"Shut up and fight, Combs!" someone yelled.

"All talk and no show. That's Jimmy!"

"Show us what 'ya got, Jimmy, or don't you never come back," another chimed in.

Frank snorted in disgust. "You talk too much to be a fighting man, bikini boy."

The crowd laughed.

"Bust 'im up, Frank!" somebody shouted.

"He's too old to fight a young guy," a woman countered.

That remark fired Jimmy up. He advanced toward Frank in bold strides. Frank opened his hands and let them hang loose at his sides. He let Jimmy spend the energy to close the distance. Without moving a muscle, Frank gave Jimmy an unnerving smile.

Jimmy faced Frank and threw the first punch, aimed at the older man's jaw. Frank grinned as he lowered his head. Jimmy pulled his fist back in pain when it hit Frank's forehead at the hairline. Frank grabbed the back of Jimmy's head with both hands and head-butted him in the nose, followed by an elbow strike to the younger man's jaw.

Jimmy's vision went dark for a second, then a wall of searing pain shot through him when Frank grabbed the front of his shirt and slammed his knee into his groin. Jimmy collapsed, nose bleeding, groaning in pain, rolling in a fetal position, holding his crotch with both hands while the crowd laughed and jeered.

A police siren in the distance drew the crowd's attention to the flashing red light on the freeway.

Frank squatted on his haunches next to Jimmy. "There's an old saying, Bikini-boy: Old age and treachery will win out over youth and skill. *You* got nothin' but youth—or what's left of it."

The pony-tailed woman handed Frank a wad of cash. "Nice work, Frank, but ya coulda played him out a little longer than ten seconds, for entertainment's sake." She looked at Renee, then at Combs, in a fetal position, groaning and cursing. "Better take your dad home, sweetie. That should be Hitchcock in the squad car."

Renee grabbed her father by the sleeve of his shirt. "Let's split, Dad, before the police get here." She ushered him to the front passenger seat of his car, then hurried to get behind the wheel. She dropped the gear shift of the Buick LeSabre into drive and took a different route out to avoid passing the police cruiser.

"I'd like to meet Hitchcock, just to shake his hand. Read about him in the paper all the time," Frank mumbled, looking back over his shoulder.

"Another time, Dad."

THE CROWD IN the parking lot parted like water for Hitchcock. He knelt beside Jimmy. "Need a doctor?" Jimmy shook his head as he grimaced in pain. "What happened here?" Jimmy shook his head again.

"This punk started something he couldn't finish, officer," someone in the crowd volunteered.

"Where's the winner, then?"

"Split before you got here," answered another bystander.

Hitchcock noticed a bulge in the right front pocket of Jimmy's slacks when he helped him to his feet.

"Show me your ID."

Jimmy refused by shaking his head.

"What's your name?"

Jimmy shook his head again.

"He's Jimmy Combs, officer," another man replied.

"Shut the hell up," Jimmy snarled, baring his teeth like a cornered animal.

"Very well, then, Jimmy Combs. You're under arrest for investigation of assault and disorderly conduct until I can figure out what happened here."

Hitchcock stood Jimmy up, handcuffed him and reached into his right front pants pocket, coming out with a handful of thin, rolled plastic baggies of white powder. Hitchcock held one up to his face.

"We'll add Investigation of Violation Uniform Controlled Substances Act to your charges. That's a felony. You can use your one free phone call at the station to call your boss. Tell him you won't be showing up for work tomorrow, or maybe the day after, or maybe years...anything is possible."

Walker rolled up in his cruiser as Hitchcock placed Jimmy in his patrol car.

"What'cha got, Roger?"

Hitchcock held up one of the cocaine bindles.

"Nice pinch, *amigo*. Need help?"

"Jimmy, here, is having a rough night. Got his butt kicked in a fight in the parking lot while I was on my way. Stay with him while I contact the bar," Hitchcock said.

Hitchcock entered the bar and scanned the crowd. He spotted the same attractive barmaid he saw last time, serving drinks to the crowd returning from watching the fight. She looked even more stunning than before in a low-cut white blouse with long puffy sleeves and a short black skirt. Her neck-length dark hair curled under in the page-boy style set off her creamy ivory skin. Their eyes met and lingered for a moment as he smiled back at her.

Seeing her a second time, looking even more alluring than before, Hitchcock wanted to know more than her name. Ralph the bartender loudly cleared his throat.

"Uh, Earth to Officer Hitchcock. What happened outside?"

He shook his head. "Uh-uh, the winner split before I arrived. I found the loser writhing in pain on the ground. I popped him for felony drug possession, thanks to the tip you gave us," he said in a confidential voice.

"Tip?" Ralph echoed. "I didn't call you guys."

"No? Who did?"

Ralph shrugged. "No clue,"

"What happened, then?"

"Jimmy's a regular here, a blow-hard used car salesman. Came in tonight claiming he won his brown belt in karate and wanted to celebrate. He ate here at the bar instead of the restaurant side and kept drinking. He hit on several women, including one who works here," Ralph said, tilting his head toward the dark-haired barmaid.

"How did it start?"

"Jimmy sat at the bar, ogling a pretty young gal sitting in a window booth with her dad. He went to their table and must have insulted them because the dad got out of the booth and squared off with him. A shoving match escalated. I threatened to call you guys if they didn't take their scuffle outside. Must have been a short fight."

"Guess so. The call came in as a guy at the counter selling drugs."

"Come to think of it, I did see Jimmy did go to the men's' room a lot. Anyway, witnesses say the older guy went through 'Brown-belt Jimmy' like Patton's army rolling through Germany."

"So, who's the winner, Ralph?"

Ralph smirked as he held up a pot of coffee. "Want some? It's still hot."

"I thought you liked me."

He turned around, his eyes searching for the pretty barmaid until they found her looking at him with eyes that all but winked as she cleared a table. He grinned slightly with an even slighter nod of thanks. With a nod of her head that meant 'you're welcome,' she smiled back.

He returned to Walker, still in his cruiser.

"Well, did Roger fall in love again tonight?"

"Hush up. I was working."

"Don't gimme that. I saw her through the window. She's a looker. Built like a–a brick house. Anyway, I did your work for you. Your boy Jimmy Combs, is a collector."

"A collector?"

"Of failure-to-appear warrants. Eight, all confirmed."

"Music to my ears," Hitchcock said absently as he stared at the barmaid who smiled at him from the other side of the window.

Walker chuckled and shook his head. "Better take care of the injured prisoner in the back of your cruiser, Romeo."

CHAPTER ELEVEN
Following The Bread Crumbs

AFTER THE DOCS patched up Jimmy Combs's nose and hand. Hitchcock found a slip of green paper from a fortune cookie in his pants pocket during booking. He laughed out loud when he read it.

"Hey, Jimmy, get this: Your fortune says, 'The greatest danger could be your stupidity.' Where did you get this?"

Combs sat on the booking room bench, scowling as he touched his bandaged nose with his wrapped right hand. "Well *obviously* it's from some Chinese joint, officer," he said in a condescending nasal tone through his broken nose.

"Which one? Here in Eastgate?"

Combs hesitated, then nodded. "Yep," he replied, breathing through his mouth.

"Tonight?"

"Yeah, why?"

"Because your stupidity got you in trouble tonight. Pretty darn accurate for a fortune cookie," Hitchcock answered cheerfully.

"Yeah, well, that's where I ate," Combs grumbled, touching his bandaged nose.

"How was the food?"

Combs gave Hitchcock a quizzical look. "Why?"

Hitchcock couldn't wipe the mischievous grin off his face. "Because if you ate at the one in Eastgate, you may need to have your stomach pumped."

Concern flashed over Combs's face. "What's the deal?"

"Just the other night, we caught the cooks cutting up deer legs and tendons in their dishes—stripping hide and hair off with a paring knife, then right into a sizzling wok."

Hitchcock sighed as he said "Maybe after this much time, you'll be all right. But the deer around here are notorious for being infested with ticks and Lyme Disease, affecting the nerves, often doing permanent damage. You should see your doctor as soon as you can."

Combs grimaced as he rubbed his stomach. "Take me back to the hospital so they can check me out."

"Too late for that now. Sorry," Hitchcock said as he filled out the arrest form.

Jimmy's feet began fidgeting. "C'mon. Please."

Hitchcock glanced at Jimmy. "Well, maybe. But

first, tell me where you got the white powder I found in your pocket, which the state lab will tell me is cocaine, right?"

Jimmy gazed at the booking room floor and shook his head. "I'm taking the fifth, officer."

"I'll see my doctor tomorrow," Combs said as Hitchcock put him in a holding cell.

"Oh? Does your doctor make jail visits?"

"Wh-what do you mean?"

"You have to see a judge before you can get out. The judge sets the bail. You post the bail, then you can get out, pending trial. Takes two, three days," Hitchcock said, faking sadness.

"So I could die in jail! Let me out so I can see my doctor. Please!"

"Think white powder, and Great Wall, Jimmy," Hitchcock said.

He called the state trooper at the State Patrol station in Bellevue.

"Hitchcock, Bellevue PD, here. Checking to see if there are any results on the blood work on the biker who was involved in the accident on the freeway."

The rookie state trooper replied true to the stiff, formal manner taught in their academy. "Yes, officer. Glad you called. Mister Piper's blood alcohol was point oh-nine percent, and his blood tested positive for cocaine. We're taking him to the King County Jail in Seattle in a few moments."

He almost laughed at the trooper's referring to an outlaw biker as "Mister."

"No surprise there. Did he say where he had been before the accident?"

"Yes, officer. Mister Piper told me he left some Chinese joint but couldn't remember the name of it. He had seven hundred dollars in fifties and hundreds, all new bills, in his wallet."

"Did he say where he was drinking and doping?"

"Yes. Mr. Piper said he did both at the Chinese place. When I pressed him for more details, he declined."

Hitchcock got the biker's full name, date of birth and address from the trooper and thanked him before ending the call.

Eastgate seemed like a ghost town with lights and wet streets when he returned from taking Jimmy to jail in Seattle. He checked parking lots and closed businesses along both sides of the freeway for the last hour of his workweek. Eastgate was quiet, but thoughts of lethal drugs coming out of The Great Wall, and the new barmaid at The Wagon Wheel raced in his mind.

CONNECTING THE DOTS now implicated Juju Kwan as the source for two unrelated men to have purchased and possessed cocaine at the same place and time. Hitchcock wondered if Combs, the dealer and Piper, the biker, know each other. Were they at The Great Wall at the same time that night? Both men have criminal histories involving drug offenses, but they seem too different to associate or be acquainted with each other, yet both knew where to go and who to see.

Adding Combs and Piper to hitman Colin Wilcox, who also had ties to The Great Wall, intensified the spotlight of suspicion of Juju Kwan.

Other observations after a year of working in Eastgate convinced Hitchcock that The Great Wall was a storefront for organized crime. Except on rare occasions, employees outnumbered customers, hours of operation were erratic, overhead exceeded income, making other sources of revenue necessary to keep the doors open.

While converging circumstances implicated The Great Wall and its owner as the drivers of narcotics trafficking, they fell short of sufficient probable cause to support investigative arrests. All of it could be explained away by even a cheap attorney and dismissed by a judge.

Not having a narcotics unit with trained undercover officers and informants after so many drug overdose cases was hurting the public, especially the young. The volume of other drug-related crimes that weren't dealt with amounted to criminal neglect by the city, in Hitchcock's mind.

He knew from his experiences in Southeast Asia that

prostitution and gambling often went hand-in-hand in opium dens but Hitchcock had never seen the slightest indication of either of those vices at The Great Wall. Perplexed and frustrated, he had no choice but to stay on alert, wait and watch for openings—while young people die or become ruined by addiction.

He shook his head at the scope of destruction the hidden powers-that-be were inflicting on the people he swore to protect—people of his hometown. For a rookie patrolman on an inexperienced small-town police department to stop ruthless, sophisticated criminals seemed far-fetched. He wondered if he was on a fool's errand.

THE NEXT DAY, his day off, after much thought, he resolved to press on, as best he could, in spite of his inexperience and his Department's shortcomings. He doubled the amount of ammunition he expended in weekly practice and bought a more powerful pair of binoculars before starting another workweek.

Then, in the back of his mind, he sensed opposition of a different kind was coming.

CHAPTER TWELVE
The War Comes Home

THE ENVELOPE IN his inbox was marked URGENT. The seal was intact. He recognized the writing as he slipped it inside his shirt and headed for the squad room. Sergeant Breen stopped him in the hallway. His expression was grave.

"Lieutenant Bostwick wants to see you in his office after shift briefing. Didn't say what for."

At Breen's words, Hitchcock flashed back in time to bouncing along a rutted jungle road in an Army jeep driven by a lieutenant, to a village near their base in Phu Loi.

The lieutenant, the MD in charge of Hitchcock's medical unit told him, "we're on a special mercy mission." He wondered why the lieutenant was smirking.

Stray goats, and pigs scattered as they arrived in a small village of grass shacks. Lieutenant Windsor led him into a grass-roofed hut, which was dark inside despite the bright afternoon sun. The stench of sweat and stale food smote his nostrils. The sight of six or seven half-dressed teenage girls lined up, facing their visitors, frightened, crowded together, so ashamed, sickened him. An adult Vietnamese woman, gaunt, missing teeth and sickly looking, smiled and bowed before the lieutenant.

"You like different girl today, Loo-tenant, sir?"

The lieutenant tilted his head toward Hitchcock. "Take care of my friend first, Mama-san, pick a girl for him," he said in his thick upper-crust Boston, accent with shortened vowels and curled r's.

From the group of sullen little girls, the wretched hag took one by the arm and brought her to Hitchcock, a scrawny girl, pitiful and helpless, in her early teens, if that. Barefoot, dressed only in a dirty silk rag that had once been a dress, which covered little of her, she stared at the dirt floor, shamed, dejected and helpless, without hope.

"She nice, yes? She orphan. Her father, soldier–die helping Americans fight communists. She yours, you take," the madam said, pushing the girl to him and pointing to a cot behind a multi-colored curtain.

Hitchcock's heart broke at the sight of her; a poor, miserable orphan.

Lieutenant Windsor laughed as he drew another sullen girl-child to himself. "What's the matter,

Hitchcock, got something against brown skin? Try it! Your girl back home won't know."

His boss, an officer whom the code of military conduct required him to salute and address as "sir," was a pervert, a sexual predator of orphans. *Officer or not, the lieutenant deserves to die,* he decided. As Hitchcock fought the desire to give the Lieutenant the death penalty issued by his bare fists, an even greater shock came.

The vile shrew exposed her mouth of mostly missing teeth in a wicked smile as she cackled and extended her bony hand to the lieutenant, who produced from his pants pocket not money, but two sealed vials, the labels of which Hitchcock recognized as morphine from the base dispensary. These pain meds, meant for wounded soldiers, would go to the enemy. Before he lost control and killed the lieutenant on the spot, Hitchcock bolted.

He leaped into the Army jeep and sped through mud puddles and deep ruts in the road without regard for enemy snipers or buried mines back to Phu Loi, alone, in uniform, risking death or capture, armed only with his personal .38 revolver in a shoulder holster.

The base commander disbelieved his report and ordered the MPs to arrest him.

"Check the dispensary, sir. You'll find at least two vials of morphine and probably other drugs are missing," he said as the MP's led him away in handcuffs and locked him in the brig.

Hours later two MPs and a captain brought Lieutenant Windsor back in handcuffs. The arrogant air of superiority the enlisted men knew him for was gone. He had been caught. His hatred of Hitchcock, as pure as a flame, was all Windsor had left. The MPs placed him in the cell next to Hitchcock.

At that second a demonic aspect came over Windsor, the like of which Hitchcock had never seen. His face became blood-red and contorted, blue veins bulged on his forehead, ready to burst. His eyes bulged and whites of them turned blood red. He stared at Hitchcock and gripped the iron bars between them. In a raspy, hissing voice Hitchcock did not recognize, Lieutenant Windsor said "I will *get* you for this, Hitchcock, damn you! I will *get* you!"

Hitchcock stared at Windsor, shocked beyond speech. Out of the blue he finally said, "I know who and what you really are, Lieutenant." The words that came out of his mouth surprised him. They were calm and deliberate, authoritative. Where they came from, he didn't know, but they disarmed Windsor. His appearance and mood returned to normal and he sat meekly on his bunk, saying nothing more.

Two days later the MPs removed Hitchcock from his cell. The captain informed him that their investigation cleared him of any wrongdoing and ordered him to pack and wait for new orders. He was free to relax on the base until then.

The uncertainty of where he was going next made him nervous. It didn't look like the two-week leave he was due for would happen. He read books, wrote letters to his mother and sisters, ate and slept.

A week later a helicopter flew him to a special operations unit in another part of the country. The last he saw of Phu Loi was from the air. Thus began his secret second tour in and out of Vietnam for another year.

Despite a second tug on his sleeve from Sergeant Breen, Hitchcock's flashback continued. More pain medications–morphine and other drugs–were discovered to be missing from the dispensary safe and later found in Lieutenant Windsor's locker. An investigation revealed he had indeed been black-marketing drugs intended for wounded soldiers, knowing the narcotics went to the enemy. The military tribunal sentenced Windsor to the Leavenworth federal prison, where he later succumbed to paralytic dementia and cerebral atrophy resulting from late-stage syphilis.

Hitchcock felt a third, sharper tug on his sleeve as a voice said, "Hey Roger, you all right?" Sergeant Breen asked.

He shook himself. "Sorry, I guess I zoned out, Sarge."

"You sure did. The second I told you Bostwick wants to see you, your mind went somewhere else. You *sure* you're all right?"

He flashed an apologetic grin at Sergeant Breen. "I'm fine. Something else came to mind while you were talking and I got distracted."

"Attend shift briefing, then see Lieutenant Bostwick," Breen said.

NERVOUS ABOUT NOT knowing what to expect from Lieutenant Bostwick, Hitchcock took his seat with the other officers in the smoke-filled squad room, where Sergeant Breen held a smoldering cigarette between his fingers as he read the latest bulletin.

"All right, listen up," Breen began. "We're gonna have a busy night. But first off, there's this, and it hasn't been released to the public yet. The Coroner's office called this afternoon. The decomposed body of a white male found by a couple deer hunters in the woods near the Issaquah-Hobart Road three days ago has been positively identified as that of Colin Wilcox, the convicted killer Hitchcock arrested at Charlie's Place. The cause of death was a bullet to the back of the head. His hands were bound behind him. The County dicks are investigating but since Wilcox was our arrest, we will continue our investigation as it pertains to us."

A wave of bitter muttering about the city council and the manager's aides being pussies in striped pants and no range to practice in wafted through the squad room.

Sergeant Breen turned to Hitchcock. "Roger, you are

to meet with county homicide dicks and ours at Captain Holland's office at eight o'clock Monday morning. It's about your arrest of Wilcox."

Returning his attention to his squad, Breen said, "Got us a full moon tonight. The animals are tearing the city apart. Second shift has been swamped since sundown. Get your gear and hit the street. It's gonna be a long night. Back each other up. I don't want anybody getting hurt. Diss-*missed!*"

Hitchcock remained seated as the squad filed out of the squad room, mulling over the news of Wilcox's execution. Nothing made sense–stakes so high as to warrant a death sentence to ensure silence didn't figure with a blue-collar beer joint like Charlie's.

The meaning of the place and manner of the execution wasn't lost on him, but homegrown Americans who hadn't been where he'd been would miss it. *The people behind this are foreigners. Asian foreigners who proved by staging the body this way that they don't understand American culture,* he realized.

The villages he saw on patrols where the Viet Cong had executed leaders came to mind. Their bodies were staged their bodies in the same way as Wilcox as a warning against cooperating with the Americans or their allies. He interpreted the staging of Wilcox's body here as an announcement that there's a new wolf in the sheep pen.

He remembered the Army developed intelligence

on enemy movements and strengths by building trust with the civilian populace. As a result of food, medical services and protection freely given, poor villagers who came to Phu Loi gave the Army the information they needed to take the fight to the enemy. Battles were won, lives were saved.

As a police officer, he would have to do the same if he expected to be effective against the influx of dangerous drugs. He needed a mouse-in-the-corner, a mole–at least one would increase his effectiveness and the safety of the people.

He shook his head in disgust and dismay when he thought of the leaders upstairs. A *criminal intelligence unit like Seattle PD has is needed, and we don't even have a narcotics unit.*

HE READ THE envelope in his shirt. It was unsigned but he recognized the writing. He found Walker in the hallway.

"I need a favor, Ira. I'm to meet Bostwick in his office now. I've been warned it's a set-up. I need you to stand outside the door and witness everything that's said. Don't get caught."

Walker seemed surprised but he didn't hesitate. "Sure thing," he replied.

He had never dealt with Lieutenant Bostwick before, yet a strange sense of *déjà vu* came over him as he walked the twenty or so steps down the hall to the lieutenant's office. He remembered Walker's warning that Bostwick pushed hard for the review board to fail him on his probationary first year. The why of it was a mystery, but it didn't matter now.

In appearance, mannerisms, East Coast accent and arrogance, Bostwick mirrored Lieutenant Windsor.

As he knocked on Lieutenant Bostwick's office door, his mind saw Lieutenant Windsor coming across the miles of time for revenge.

"Come in, Roger," he heard the lieutenant say.

Like a little boy trying to wear big pants, the balding weasel whom the line officers hated had come to the station on a Saturday, off-duty, his uniform perfectly creased, the brass of his badge, gun belt buckle, shirt buttons, and collar bars gleaming, to attack a rookie patrolman. He didn't even look up when Hitchcock entered.

"Sit down," he ordered in an officious tone, as he continued poring over his papers.

"Thanks, Lieutenant, but I'll stand. What do you want, sir?"

Bostwick looked up, shocked. A rookie had seized the whip hand of rank and authority from him in seconds. Embarrassed and flustered by such a quick turning of tables, he coughed to buy time.

"Yes, well, uh, this isn't Chicago, New York, or LA, Hitchcock," Bostwick began timidly. "This is Bellevue. Nothing ever happens here. Some citizens complained to me about your beating up this poor Indian fellow from the woods around Carnation–Beecham, I think his name is. I want to hear what you have to say for yourself, apart from your report."

He calmly shook his head. "Everything I have to say is in my report, sir."

"I've read the medical reports," Bostwick said, his tone icy and condescending. "Beecham and McMinn were hospitalized by you and Officer Joel Otis. Otis being the one who used his baton per our regulations. Beecham, the one *you* fought, or I should say 'assaulted,' received a broken nose, a fractured and dislocated jaw, and a bruised sternum. He eats and drinks through a straw because his jaw is wired shut. You did all this with just your fists, I understand?"

"That is correct, sir."

"How amazing…and disgusting," Bostwick said snottily. "Did you *ever* tell him he was under arrest, Hitchcock?"

"No need, sir."

"No need?" Bostwick said, pretending to be shocked.

"No sir," Hitchcock replied, "there was no need to tell him that because he was assaulting another officer when I arrived at the scene."

Bostwick rose from his chair and walked around his desk. Eyes gleaming with hate, he glared up at Hitchcock, hands on his hips, his pudgy body sharply contrasting with Hitchcock's lean athleticism.

"So instead of talking to him you just beat him up as soon as you arrived. Didn't you have your baton with you?"

"*Of course,* I had my baton, sir."

"But you used your fists instead. Why?"

"Beecham was barehanded, sir. Rather than escalate the fight by using a weapon, I subdued him bare-handed."

"Oh, yes, of course. I read in the paper about your boxing career. Over a hundred fights, mostly wins. You made the U.S. Olympics team. How impressive."

Hitchcock held to an even tone of voice and manner. He didn't yield to anger or righteous indignation. "Thank you, sir," he said.

Bostwick's eyes narrowed. "But isn't boxing out of place for someone of your station, a doctor's son, from a respectable family? You are white, Hitchcock, so how could you handle being around *neeee-groes*?" he demanded, scowling.

Remembering what the anonymous note said, Hitchcock didn't take the bait. Instead, he smiled as he said, "It was a wonderful maturing experience, sir. They accepted me after I won respect on their terms. As a white kid from Bellevue, they thought of me as soft and weak until I proved myself otherwise. I'm still friends with several of my former teammates."

Bostwick's face reddened with contempt.

Hitchcock had heard rumors about Bostwick's sheltered upbringing, elite private schools, tutors, and guarded social life. It was common knowledge on the Department that though in his early thirties, he had never married, and never attended Department social functions.

For other reasons, he regarded Bostwick as an enigma. Since coming on the Department, Bostwick had been kept in administrative positions. Except for one situation where he was called to pick up a shoplifter from the store detective at the Nordstrom Best store in Bellevue Square, he had never made an arrest or written a traffic citation, yet he swiftly rose to the rank of lieutenant.

"And what about your service in Vietnam, Hitchcock? Over half of your time there is classified,' Bostwick sneered. "How many people did you kill? Any of them babies?"

Hitchcock was losing respect for Bostwick by the second. The anonymous letter under his shirt was right – Bostwick had been coached to say things regarding race and military service to provoke him.

"You won't answer," Bostwick continued. "Probably because you killed babies there. And here you are, with a gun and a badge..."

As Hitchcock kept himself in check, Bostwick began to boil as his provocations became louder and shriller yet without effect.

"When I become Chief, none of you veterans will be here. You're all dangerous, all liable to go on a rampage any time. What do you say to *that*, Hitchcock?"

This was the bait the note warned him about. He smiled for effect and shrugged his shoulders. "Why, nothing, sir," he replied.

Bostwick's flaccid jowls reddened and shook as he said, "And officers won't have guns. Neither would citizens when I'm Chief. When I worked the front desk as sergeant, I refused citizen renewals of concealed weapons permits. 'Nope!' I told them, 'you don't need a gun,'" he said in a shrill voice and an emphatic wave of his delicate hands. "What do you think of *that*, Hitchcock?"

He looked at Bostwick. "Since you asked, I think you put your personal biases ahead of your duty. Sir."

Entering another stage of unraveling, Bostwick raised his voice to a near shout." I-I'm going to put a letter in your file regarding y-your use of excessive f-force and f-failure to follow p-p-procedures!" He stammered.

Hitchcock said nothing.

"You should quit and join a big city department! Rough types like you d-don't b-belong here among decent respectable people in this quiet community."

Hitchcock still said nothing. Inwardly he wanted to give Bostwick the thrashing he deserved, but the discipline instilled in him from boxing and the military enabled him to endure baseless attacks.

Bostwick returned to his chair and leaned back, clasping his hands behind his head, trying his best to smirk as a last-ditch effort to gain a psychological advantage over Hitchcock. "Well? What do you have to say? Gonna quit? I hear Seattle's hiring again!"

Maintaining a serene stance, Hitchcock replied "With all due respect *to your rank*, Lieutenant, I am one hundred percent in the right. Two officers and an officer's wife were beaten and bleeding on the ground when I arrived. The officer with me was struck down in seconds. Beecham was beating and kicking Mark Forbes when I stopped him with no more force than necessary."

Bostwick's mouth dropped open. He leaned forward in his chair. "Forbes, you say?"

"That's right, Lieutenant. Mark Forbes would have died or become a vegetable if I didn't physically stop Beecham when I did. Now, Lieutenant, who are the citizens who say I beat Beecham up? What are their names and where are their statements? I want to read them!"

Hitchcock waited, but Bostwick said nothing.

"I see," Hitchcock said after waiting. "You're lying. There are no witnesses. Go ahead and write your letter, I will appeal it. I've had enough of your toothless threats. Dispatch is holding calls for me."

Bostwick shot out of his chair, his double chin quivering like jelly. Pointing at the door, he stamped his foot on the carpet and shouted, "Out! Get out! Get out! You–you! I'll *get* you for this! I'll *get* you for insubordination and excessive force. *Then* we'll see how long you stay here!"

Hitchcock, showing complete self-possession by his indifference to his persecutor's wild animosity, calmly stared at Bostwick as he heard himself repeat the same words he'd spoken years earlier: *"I know who and what you really are, Lieutenant."*

In a stunning departure from his previous, heated behavior, Bostwick stared past Hitchcock at the wall, saying nothing, exactly as Lieutenant Windsor had done three years earlier.

Hitchcock joined Walker in the hall. Neither spoke until they reached the parking lot.

Walker tilted his head back, hooting with laughter. "Hooo-wee! I heard the whole thing! Bostwick's a 220!" he said, stating the local cop slang for a crazy person. "*Gotta* be the full moon. But—how did you know to ask me to be a witness for you?"

Hitchcock handed him the note. Walker inspected the writing in the moonlight, then sniffed it. "Perfume! Ahh! A woman wrote this. One with class!" His eyes popped when he read it.

"Wow! Bostwick, who struts around here like a Nazi is a spy for the third floor of City Hall! No signature, of course. Yep, this is somebody in position to hear schemes being hatched, who went to great risk to warn you. This is someone who *really* likes you."

Walker playfully pushed his hat back on his head, held the note up to eye level and rubbed his chin, pretending to be in deep thought. "Hmm...now-let-me-think," he said with a wink. "Knowing you, the writer is in love with you. Ah, yes, it's the fox in the prosecutor's office. Eve, right?"

Hitchcock snatched the note back. "Bostwick might lie about our meeting. I need you to write a memo on what you heard. Date it and then hold on to it."

"Sure," Walker chuckled, shaking his head. "Glad to. Imagine: that the little Nazi Boast-vich is a backstabber, we already knew, but he's a 220 too!"

"And keep quiet about me and Eve."

"Eve who?"

IN HIS OFFICE, Lieutenant Bostwick paced, his flabby fists clenched, muttering to himself, his face reddening, looking down. He stopped pacing, tilted his head back, shut his eyes, opened wide his mouth, and let loose a long guttural scream, a primeval howl from a dark dimension of the man shook the window of his office. Then came another, even louder, more guttural and plaintive than the first, which terrified the clerks across the hall.

IN THE STATION parking lot, the same powerful wave of triumph Hitchcock experienced after hard-won victories in boxing washed over him as he buckled the seat belt of his cruiser. He had fought and won against evils past, present, and future.

Thoughts of his possibilities with the buxom barmaid at The Wagon Wheel filled his mind as he left the station, followed by thoughts of Eve, the Scandinavian beauty in the prosecutor's office whose timely written warning saved his career tonight. *Ah, then there's Rhonda, my cowgirl ER doc, and of course, there's Allie the little waitress. What's the old saying? "So many women, so little time?"*

He cruised through the moonlight and shadows along Richards Road toward Eastgate, thinking about his dog, Jamie, faithfully guarding his cabana in the deep woods, so isolated and private, only two minutes from the station. With satisfaction he thought about the strong bond he enjoyed with Otis, Sherman and Walker, all deliberate men.

CRACKLING RADIO STATIC suddenly interrupted his reverie. The voice of the dispatcher came through. *"Three Zero Six, respond Code Two to back up Three Zero Five on a Domestic Violence in progress at 11474 SE 36th Place. Woman reports husband is drunk, has beaten her. She reports head injuries. Be advised—the husband was arrested last month on a DV call at the same address for assault, assaulting an officer and resisting arrest. An officer was injured."*

Hitchcock's pulse quickened. *Three Zero Five is Tom*

Sherman! He grabbed his radio mic, "Are there firearms in the house?"

"We asked, but the line went dead before the woman answered."

"Call the woman back. We need to know."

"We tried. No answer," the dispatcher replied.

"On my way. ETA three minutes."

Adrenaline surged through him as he flipped the switch for his roof-mounted red emergency light and accelerated. His peripheral vision narrowed as he weaved along the curves of Richards Road as fast as he dared.

Sherman's voice came on the air: *"Expedite. I'm across the street. Heard a scream and a loud crash in the house. Now it's silent."*

Hitchcock floored the accelerator. The increased speed caused him to cross the centerline. Fortunately, there was no other traffic on the dark winding curves, lighted only by patches of moonlight peeking through the trees.

He clicked his radio mic: "ETA two minutes..."

ACKNOWLEDGEMENTS

Special thanks to various members of the Bellevue and Seattle Police Departments with whom I served for twenty-one years, for their contributions to this series.

ABOUT THE AUTHOR

JOHN HANSEN draws from personal experience for most of his writing. Between 1966-1970 he served as a Gunners Mate aboard an amphibious assault ship that ran solo missions in and out of the rivers and waterways of South Vietnam and other places.

While a patrol officer with the Bellevue Police Department, his fellow officers nicknamed him "Mad Dog" for his tenacity. After ten years in Patrol, he served eleven years as a detective, investigating homicide, suicide, robbery, assault, arson and rape cases.

As a private investigator since retirement, his cases have taken him across the United States and to other countries and continents. He is the winner of several awards for his books, short stories and essays.